TOMORROW'S WORLD:

Darkly Humorous Tales from the Future

Tomorrow's World

Guy Portman

FOREWORD

I've known Guy Portman for nearly thirty years. In those days, cutting-edge technology for us was playing solitaire on the school computer. Since then, a lot has changed. Smartphones. Social Media. Caitlyn Jenner. But some things haven't, like Guy's sardonic wit and healthy cynicism for humanity's pretensions and peccadilloes. A keen social observer, it seems obvious now that he was destined to write a hilarious satire about the next 180 years.

Because in *Tomorrow's World*, Guy has seen the writing on the wall. And it's in emojis. Through short scenes flipping between various levels of society, we're taken year by year through a future full of psychotic capitalism, hyper-branding and extreme virtual reality. This is a world not a million miles removed from our own, where celebrities are worshipped like gods, drones are as common as pigeons and life expectancies for the rich are becoming biblical. You thought people were pissed off with the 1%? Just wait until you see how they react to the 0.1%.

Like all great visionary satires, the book takes our current foibles and obsessions to their logical, gruesome and absurd conclusions. And it'll make you laugh out loud along the way. That's because Guy's particular vein of dark humour is on show in each prescient and deadpan vignette. These are not just about our near future. By giving us caustic glimpses through the best part of two hundred years of political, social and cultural upheaval, *Tomorrow's World* is constantly evolving. In essence, it's a warning about the ramifications of a grotesquely ageing population, as demonstrated by recurring characters Walter and Terrence: American plutocrat and British worker respectively. It may be great living to over 150. But how would you feel if you had to work for an extra half a century or so?

We're in an era of ever-shortening attention spans. For example, I just checked Twitter twelve times while writing that sentence. Fortunately, this book is the perfect antidote. As well as being a quick, exciting, provocative read, like flash fiction collected into a coherent novel, *Tomorrow's World* is also a plea to put down the VR headset and experience life directly. Because nothing lasts forever. Except maybe solitaire.

Adam Riley
Comedian

I: STATE OF PLAY

DEMOCRACY

JUNE 3RD, 2071 AD - 18C CLAYTON CRESCENT, BASINGSTOKE - ENGLAND - A woman is experiencing a comedy sketch on her holovision. One of the comedians says, 'Not long to go now until the general election. Who will you vote for?'

'Bank.'

'And you?'

'Financial institution.'

'How about you?'

'Corporation.'

The woman snickers. She considers this to be an accurate assessment. From next door comes the sound of a raised male voice. The woman surmises that her neighbour Terrence must be engaging in one of his online, dating-style role-play games. She turns the holovision's volume up.

Virtual Reality

ONE YEAR LATER – 18B CLAYTON CRESCENT, BASINGSTOKE –
Strutting across the living room floor is 25-year-old Terrence. He
is wearing a virtual-reality headset and matching goggles. These
have allowed him to swap the drab confines of his living room for
a trendy bar, where young women are perched along its counter,
sipping vividly coloured cocktails. They, like Terrence, are real
people, adopting glamorous, fictional online identities: blending
their own personas with fiction.

Terrence passes a hand through his swept-back, virtual blond
hair before pushing out his virtual muscular chest, which is
accentuated by a virtual tight T-shirt. At the bar a woman is
watching him out of the corner of her eye. When Terrence
swaggers up to her, he says, 'Do I come here often?'

'Twat.'

Unfazed, Terrence grabs a mojito from the barman and struts
off. A woman swivels on her stool to face him. Terrence says, 'I'd
really like to see how you look when I'm naked.'

At the far end of the counter is a buxom young blonde with
long, silky hair. Having sauntered nonchalantly past her, Terrence
turns to her and says, 'Do you believe in love at first sight or
should I walk past you again?'

DISPUTED ISLAND

THE FOLLOWING YEAR – JULY 19TH, 2073 AD – TERRACOTTA STATE DRAWING ROOM – 10 DOWNING STREET, LONDON – ENGLAND – The Prime Minister is slouched on a sofa, experiencing an England cricket test match. He is oblivious to the room's ringing holophone.

An aide knocks on the door, opens it slightly and peeks into the room's interior. Seeing the Prime Minister on the sofa she hurries towards him, calls his name several times and, getting no response, nudges him on the shoulder. Having taken off his virtual-reality helmet the Prime Minister says, 'This better be important. Can't you see I'm experiencing the cricket?'

'Everyone's trying to get hold of you. Didn't you hear the holophone ringing?'

'Of course not; I was absorbed in the cricket.'

'I'm the bearer of bad news,' says the aide. 'Very bad news.'

'Well, go on, what is it?'

'The Chinese Armada has been spied off the south coast.'

'Oh no!'

'They're heading towards the disputed Isle of Wight.'

'Disputed? Ludicrous. The Isle of Wight is nowhere near China.'

'When has that ever stopped them?'

'I know what to do,' says the Prime Minister. 'I'll send the mighty British Navy to intercept them.'

'The what?'

'The British Navy. The pride of the seas.'

'That was well over a century ago. Nowadays our navy is smaller than Uganda's.'

'Don't be ridiculous; Uganda is landlocked.'

'I know.'

CALL TO PRAYER

NOVEMBER 5TH, 2074 AD – LEINES, THE ARCTIC CIRCLE – NORWAY – A tourist is gawping in wonder at the alluring pale pink and green nebulous bands illuminating the night sky. These are the *aurora borealis* (Northern Lights).

The tourist, hearing a sonorous chanting echoing through the fjord, cups a hand to their ear.

'Hayya 'alas-salah, Hayya 'alas-salah.

Hayya 'alal-falah, Hayya 'alal-falah.'

The tourist, tugging on their guide's sleeve, says, 'Listen! What's that chanting sound?'

'The Islamic call to prayer.'

DATING

SEPTEMBER 13TH, 2075 AD – COVENT GARDEN, LONDON – Terrence's ability to stimulate his virtual dates using teledildonics (remote mutual masturbation – tactile sensations communicated via a data link) has resulted in him acquiring the moniker Titillating Terrence. But that is in the virtual world, not the real one, where he is now, sitting in a café waiting for his date to arrive.

Terrence clasps his trembling hands together. He is acutely aware that he is now plain Terrence, a 28-year-old virgin with no real-time dating experience. Last week he met his date briefly in a virtual-reality hangout. Though surprised when she suggested a real-time date, he had nonchalantly agreed.

A young woman in a thigh-length skirt enters the café and scans the interior. She scowls when she sees Terrence, the only lone man on the premises. She raises an eyebrow when she points in his direction.

'Yo!' calls out Terrence in as confident a voice as he can muster. 'Are you Lavinia49?'

'It's Lavinia. Lavinia49 is my online alias. Nice to meet you, TitillatingTerrence_DJ.'

'Hi.'

'Your real name is just Terrence, isn't it?'

'Um, yes.'

She pulls out a seat and sits down. The pair study the café's menu in awkward silence. Terrence, peeping at her over the top of his menu, considers that, though marginally pudgier than in virtual reality, she looks pretty good.

'A caffè latte with synthetic milk,' says Lavinia to the waitress. 'Make doubly sure it's not real milk; I can't stand cruelty to cows.'

'Will do. And you?'

7

'The same,' says Terrence, who had been poised to order a caffè latte with real milk.

The waitress departs.

'So, what do you do, Terrence?'

'Virtual-reality gaming and—'

'I meant for a job.'

'I am employed by a car park company, in err ... Basingstoke.' Terrence feels heat rising to his cheeks. 'We have err ... spaces for 30,000 vehicles.'

'What do you do there?'

'Um, correlating data and analysing stuff.'

'What stuff?'

'Which spaces are the most used and at what times of day. There is a great deal of quantitative and qualitative reporting. It's um ... very—'

'I work in textile design. And I really like it.'

As she proceeds to talk at great length about her job, Terrence notes that she unfolds her arms for the first time since she sat down. Having conducted some research on body language prior to this date, he considers this good news.

'Contributing to a greener environment is the most important thing in my life,' she says. 'That is why I chose my current employer.'

'I see,' says Terrence, who now takes a sip of his caffè latte with synthetic milk.

'I've got a good idea! You ask me a question and I will answer, then I'll do the same. It will be fun.'

'Um ... put in order of preference the following err ... four historical artificial sweeteners: aspartame, saccharin, sucrose and err ... sucralose.'

Lavinia raises her eyebrows. Terrence is aware from his research that this is a flirtatious body language signal.

'Sucrose is my fave, followed by saccharin and sucralose. Aspartame is like so wrong and has done so much damage to people in poor countries. I don't even want to go there. Now it's my turn. Tell me about a time when you made a suggestion at work that was really appreciated?'

Terrence, looking up at the ceiling, ponders his response.

'Actually, I am going to answer that question. Last month our design team was planning a sustainable, eco-friendly, environmentally sound clothesline, redesigned for the modern world. Like, the most amazing thing happened, because I just happened to walk into my boss's office and ...'

Examining his date's smiling visage, blinking eyes and exuberant gesturing, Terrence senses the time is right to move to the next stage. This usually entails bringing the teledildonics into play. He scans the table.

'My boss said my idea was the best thing she had heard in like ages. And guess what?' Lavinia's gaze is fixed on Terrence. *Terrence picks up a teaspoon.* 'We are creating a traditional Bangladeshi-inspired clothesline.' *Terrence slips the teaspoon under the table.* 'I am so excited about this incredible project.' Her open mouth forms a wide smile. *Terrence reaches out with the spoon towards his date's bare inner thigh.* 'We are going to incorporate logos and symbols that actually inspire women, which is so ironic considering Bangladesh AHHHHHHHH!'

ICON

OCTOBER 8TH, 2076 AD – 18B CLAYTON CRESCENT, BASINGSTOKE – Terrence is alone at home, slouched on the settee, idly flicking through the channels on his holovision. He opts for the BBC News channel. A military analyst is giving their opinion on the disputed Isle of Wight situation. There has been no sighting of the Chinese Armada in months, and the analyst seems quietly confident that it should not be reappearing anytime soon.

'Good,' says Terrence, who now proceeds to flick through the channels again. He settles on an arts programme. Positioned on one side of the holovision studio is the hostess, on the other a culture and arts commentator. In between them is a hologram of a sculpture.

The hostess says, 'Please tell us about today's exhibit.'

'This iconic, triumvirate sculpture is one of the European region's most celebrated tourist attractions.'

'It reminds me of the sculptures from antiquity.'

'Obviously. Its creator is regarded as the foremost Ultra Renaissance bronze sculptor. She utilises the lost-wax casting method for much of her work. In this instance she created full-sized models of the three sculptures that make up this historic triumvirate. It is 88% copper and 12% tin.

'Note the realism in the bouffant hair and chiselled features. Here he stands in his leather jacket in front of the sports car, his feet just over shoulder-width apart, his torso tilted marginally to the left, his arms hanging at his sides, his hands relaxed yet poised.'

Now pointing at the image on the right-hand side of the triumvirate, she says, 'Here we see the icon clad only in shorts, a float held in his right hand. Note the sense of urgency in the

10

defined, taut muscles of the limbs. The image incorporates a blend of feline grace, alpha masculinity and Greek god.'

'Amazing!'

'The triumvirate's *pièce de résistance* is this magnificent centrepiece, which adeptly captures the zeitgeist of the era. It depicts the cultural icon singing into the microphone. The song is of course *Looking for Freedom*, which he sung live in Berlin in 1989, just before the Berlin Wall came down. The single topped the German charts for eight consecutive weeks.'

SEXUAL ORIENTATION

– Terrence has been toying with the idea of applying for a job at CCP (Countrywide Car Parks) for a while. He is currently filling out the required application forms. Terrence turns his attention to question seven.

7) What is your sexual orientation? Asexual – Abrosexual – Aegosexual – Autosexual – Bisexual … Heterosexual … Having selected heterosexual, Terrence continues surveying the list. Heteroflexible – Homosexual … Klismaphile.

Klismaphile. What is a klismaphile? Terrence looks up the meaning on the holonet – Sexual expression in which a person attains sexual gratification from receiving enemas (i.e. cleansing of the colonic canal via anal douching). *Here's hoping there won't be any klismaphiles at Countrywide Car Parks.*

Neusexual – Objectum-Sexual – Paedophile (note: we regretfully inform you that we do not currently have a paedophile in the workplace scheme. Selecting this option will exclude you from employment). *No skin off my nose.*

Pansexual – Polysexual – Prefer Not To Say – Psychrophile … Skoliosexual. Terrence, recollecting his sexual orientation classes back at primary school, remembers that skoliosexual is a term that refers to those who have a sexual attraction to non-binary identified individuals.

Teratophile – Transsexual – Trisexual … Virtual-Reality Sexual. Terrence is considering selecting the virtual-reality sexual option, but as he has already selected heterosexual he is unsure as to whether his potential employer will deem it acceptable to select more than one option. Terrence contemplates that perhaps the solution is to go for the 'prefer not to say' option. However, he concludes that this might be viewed as not candid. He hopes the final option on the list might offer a solution – Zoosexual.

MILITANT SECULARISATION

MARCH 7TH, 2078 AD – 10 DOWNING STREET, LONDON – 'We are a secular state,' says the Prime Minister to the male, female and transgendered ministers standing in a line in front of him. 'Can anyone remind me what the official definition of a secular state is? I can't remember.'

'Yes,' says the female minister. 'A secular state is a state that purports to be officially neutral in matters of religion, supporting neither religion nor irreligion.'

'I don't like that definition,' says the Prime Minister. 'Let's change it to – a secular state is a state that is officially neutral in matters of religion, supporting irreligion.'

'That's contradictory, Prime Minister,' says the trans minister. 'A state cannot be neutral in matters of religion if it is supporting irreligion.'

'Good point,' says the Prime Minister. 'How about this – a secular state is a state that officially demands irreligion.'

'Like France,' says the female minister.

'Whilst it pains me to defer to the French other than when it comes to cuisine and cinema, yes, we will be just like them. We hereby declare ourselves to be a secular state, like France.'

'Why are we doing this?' says the trans minister. 'Organised religion is dying just fine on its own. Government interference could reignite the whole thing again. So why don't we just stay out of it?'

'Because we must adhere to our voters' beliefs. And non-belief is the fastest growing category of belief. Has been for a century and a half,' says the Prime Minister. 'And besides, irrationality and an unscientific world view have no place in contemporary society.'

'What form are our militant, hyper, radical, or whatever you want to call them, secularising policies going to take?' asks the female minister.

'Religious symbols are to be vilified, derided and banned from the public sphere. I'm talking nothing worn on, or wrapped around heads. And no religious symbol jewellery or trinkets. Pork served in all schools. No alterative meals offered. Just like the French.'

'And beef?' says the male minister.

'What about it?'

'There's a religion that doesn't eat beef.'

'Well, we'll have compulsory beef too.'

'We could have beef on Mondays, pork on Tuesdays,' says the male minister.

'Shellfish!' says the female minister. 'There's a religion that doesn't eat shellfish.'

'No, we are not serving shellfish,' says the Prime Minister. 'The education budget doesn't stretch to shellfish; and besides, there's a high risk of food poisoning with shellfish. We could end up being sued.'

'What do we do about celebrity worshippers, Prime Minister?' asks the trans minister. 'The worship of celebrities is on the increase.'

'They're to be exempted.'

DRONES

APRIL 19TH, 2079 AD - OXFORD STREET, LONDON - Terrence is returning from his lunch break when he sees the pedestrians on the pavement ahead peering up at the sky. Thirty metres above the road an orbicular SPU delivery drone is whirring around in circles, pursued by a murder of raucously cawing crows. The drone's hatch has flapped open and the crows are trying to get inside, lured by the foodstuffs contained therein.

A crow dive-bombs through the open flap. Another follows. The drone, whirring ever faster, emits a wheezing noise as crows descend upon it and peck savagely at the exterior. A Nile drone, swerving to avoid the mayhem, beeps furiously, a row of red lights illuminating its sides. And here come the seagulls, squawking incessantly as they descend on the drone, enraging the frantic crows.

There is a collective gasp from the crowd when the drone turns upside down, the contents of its interior tumbling in a cascade down to the road. A man exclaims, '*Trucs gratuits!*' And a woman says, 'Free *nkan na!*' A youth shrieks, 'Free stuff *innit!*'

The crowd rushes into the road. Vehicles brake as the melee grabs the fallen packages. Terrence remains on the pavement, watching the pandemonium unfold.

Meanwhile, the drone crashes noisily onto the roof of the John Lewis department store, a plume of purpurescent smoke rising from the wreckage. The crows have descended on the road, and the seagulls too. Terrence sees a black-backed gull and a woman engaging in a tug of war over a large, circular Camembert cheese. When the woman beats at the gull with her designer handbag, it releases its grip on the cheese. The woman scampers away, her prize clasped under one arm.

16

Terrence notices a box of chocolates from an exclusive Regent Street Belgian chocolatier lying on the road, close to where he stands. He hurries over, grabs the chocolates, beats away the incoming crow with his forearm, hides the chocolates under his jacket, looks left and right and then dashes off in the direction of CCP headquarters.

THE COALFACE

MAY 21ST, 2080 AD – COUNTRYWIDE CAR PARKS HEADQUARTERS –
PORTMAN SQUARE, LONDON – Terrence is one of a trio of junior
data analysts who spend their days in this corner of the office. All
morning he has been comparing the success rates of the various
sensor models his company utilises to direct self-drive cars to
available parking spaces.

A sixty-something company director approaches, an R2D2-
style droid scooting along the carpet beside him. Personal
assistant droids, such as this *Stars Wars* franchise-inspired model,
are all the rage.

When the director says, 'What's up, Han Solo?' the male data
analyst on Terrence's left mutters, 'Wanker,' under his breath
before adding, 'All's good.'

When the director says, 'How are things with you, Princess Leia?',
the female analyst on Terrence's right says, 'Great,' her enthusiastic
response contrasting with her stern-looking countenance.

'And how about you, C-3PO?'

'Everything is fine,' says Terrence.

The director says, 'I need you members of the Rebel Alliance to
run the latest system update report for Greater London for me.'

The three data analysts are about to respond when the R2D2-
style droid's head rotates 180-degrees. It emits a, *WOOOAH twee-
vwoop VRrrUHD DEda dah.*

The director looks quizzically down at the droid. The noise it
emitted a moment ago is translated into English on the small blue
screens on its head. *You need manager approval to access that site.*

'Why yes, of course,' says the director. 'We better go find the
Rebel Alliance system honcho.' He walks off, R2D2 scooting
beside him.

'What a dweeb,' says the female data analyst.

'Geek,' says the male data analyst. 'Gimping around with that toy at his age. That dude's never been laid in his life, I'm telling you.'

'Oh, that's for certain,' says the female data analyst. 'His love life will consist of some sick, twisted online role-play shit.'

Terrence swallows. He stands up.

'Where you going, bro?' says the male data analyst.

'To get some tea.'

'Latte with soya milk,' says the female data analyst.

'Cappuccino, one real sugar,' says the male data analyst.

Terrence trudges across the office in the direction of the kitchen. The director, noticing him, calls out, 'Yo, C-3PO! Dark chocolate truffle mocha.'

MANTRA

OCTOBER 24TH, 2081 AD – CENTRAL PARK – NEW YORK CITY – AMERICA –Financier Walter is on his after-work run through Central Park. He is wearing an all-in-one, skin-tight, luminous-green running suit and a matching headband. On his feet are kung fu-style running shoes. While he runs, Walter recites his mantra aloud.

'I will be more successful. I will be richer. I will spend more.'

Having drawn to a halt on an expanse of grass, Walter adopts a wushu cat stance – weight on his back leg, the front leg bent slightly, big toe touching the ground, body leaning forward, spine held straight. He proceeds to kick the air repeatedly at head height, his kicking foot a blur of motion – 'Wah wah wahwahwah.'

His holophone is ringing. Walter stops kicking and answers it. A miniature hologram of one of his relatives appears.

'Yo!'

'Hello, Walter. How's everything going in the Big Apple?'

'Awesome! I am more successful than ever. Making even more money and spending like crazy. You could say I'm the embodiment of the American Dream. Check this running suit out. And these kicks. Wah wah wahwahwah.'

'Marvellous, Walter. Very impressive for a man of your age.'

'What do you mean, my age?'

'I am checking in to see if you are planning to come over to England for the family reunion in January?'

Walter considers it will be a good opportunity to show his new wife the old country, where his grandfather hailed from. He says, 'Yeah, count me in.'

When octogenarian Walter hangs up he readopts a wushu cat stance. As the grinning, ageing financier poses in this position, he relishes the prospect of boasting to his English relatives about how successful he is. Then, remembering his English relative Terrence, the grin mutates into a grimace. Walter had been decidedly unimpressed by his uncharismatic, much younger English relative on the couple of occasions he had met him. But Walter's real disdain for Terrence came about when he overheard him making a disparaging remark about his father, at his funeral. Walter proceeds to punch the air in frenetic fashion.

'Kwakwa kwakwakwa.'

FAMILY REUNION

JANUARY 4TH, 2082 AD – FORTE KITCHEN – WINCHESTER – ENGLAND – The extended family is stationed at a long dining table. Terrence had hoped to be sitting further away from his American relative. But train delays resulted in Terrence arriving late, and he was left with no choice but to take the one remaining seat, only one removed from him. Having taken a bite of organic pheasant, Terrence washes it down with a gulp of red wine. Observing surreptitiously his sinewy American relative's swept-back yellow mane and pinkish features, Terrence feels certain that the ageing financier has been experimenting with anti-ageing medications. *A quite extraordinary specimen*, considers Terrence not for the first time, as he inspects Walter's ostentatious, all-in-one, faux-snakeskin suit and what appear to be formal kung fu-style shoes.

Terrence is remembering the first time he met Walter. A child at the time, Terrence had been sitting in the corner of a room at a family function, reading a sci-fi novel by iconic leftist author China Miéville. Walter and his father had marched up to him and chastised him for reading *socialist hogwash*. They had seized the book from him and binned it. Terrence grips his fork so hard that his knuckles whiten. Having taken a deep breath, he resumes a conversation with the relative in the adjoining seat.

'The advances in data collation software in recent years have been remarkable—'

'Yo, Terrence!' calls out Walter. 'Enough with the data collation. You're boring the hell out of everyone.'

Several relatives snicker. Walter recommences regaling relatives about his recent exploits. Terrence observes Walter grip the young relative on either side of him tightly around the neck. Walter gestures with a tilt of his yellow mane in the direction of his young, blonde, buxom trophy wife on the other side of the table. He says, 'Check her out, guys. Hot, huh?'

The youngsters nod in agreement. Terrence emits a desultory sigh. In appearance at least she is his dream woman – the type he has only ever been acquainted with in the virtual world.

The wife makes a little fluttering wave of her hand. The youngsters wave back. A moment later Terrence hears Walter say, 'Remember this, dudes. It's all about visualisation, consumerism and free market capitalism. I've got this great mantra. Check it out. I will be more successful. I will be richer. I will—'

'We have had quite enough of your rampant consumerism,' interrupts Terrence. 'Relentless materialism is something we can do without.'

'Don't insult my religion, Terrence,' says Walter. 'You don't want to do that.'

'Rampant consumerism is not a religion.'

'Damn right it is. We've been practising rampant consumerism for over a century.'

'Easy!' calls out a relative.

'Calm down, the both of you,' says another.

'Where I come from, Terrence,' says Walter, 'the free exercise of religion is enshrined in the First Amendment.'

'Using the First Amendment to support your farcical excuse for a religion is absurd,' says Terrence. 'The majority of your countrymen are suffering as a result of your rampant consumerism.'

'Here in the developing world, you militant secularists might be stomping on folks' religious freedoms, but don't be doing it to me.'

'Leave it!' says a female relative rising to her feet.

Walter falls silent. Terrence takes a bite of organic pheasant followed by another gulp of wine. A moment later Walter says, 'Yo, Terrence.'

'Yes.'

'A little birdy tells me that you're really into virtual-dating role-play. That true?'

'No, not really.'

Terrence feels heat rising to his cheeks. He has a gulp of wine, wills Walter not to say anything more.

'So,' says Walter, 'you're telling us you're done with all that.'

'Ah, yes, pretty much.'

'So, what are you doing for kicks, now you're done with the teledildonics?'

Someone says, 'Teledildonics is not a subject for the dinner table, Walter!'

'There are youngsters here,' says someone else. 'They don't need to be hearing about 'em.'

Terrence wishes he had not confided in a relation about his extracurricular activities, for they have evidently mentioned them to Walter.

'Hey, honeybun,' calls out Walter to his wife on the opposite side of the table, 'what do you know about the tele unmentionables?'

'Nothing,' says Walter's wife.

'Well,' says Walter, 'Terrence is the man to enlighten you.'

Walter's wife says, 'I don't want to know.'

Terrence wishes the ground would swallow him up. Walter's wife is staring at him. The smile that graced her pretty countenance all lunch is gone, and the corners of her mouth are now curving abruptly downwards. Terrence, picking up a bottle of wine, says, 'More wine anyone?'

Party Time

JULY 21ST, 2083 AD – WARWICKSHIRE – ENGLAND – The self-drive car turns off the A435, accelerates down the lane, swerves around a corner and glides to a halt outside a warehouse. The car's occupants, a boyfriend and girlfriend, clamber out onto the grass, where they stand, mouths agape, listening to the blaring hyper-trance emanating from the party.

'That bass is booming,' says the boy. 'It's going to be frantic in there.'

'Craving that hyper-trance sound,' says the girl. 'Can't wait to get in there and see and feel it.'

And then the boy utters the immortal words. The very same words uttered by his ancestors, who stood as they do now, outside the warehouses that housed the rave parties of the 1990s. He says, 'Let's get fucked.'

The interior is packed with rabid revellers dancing frenziedly, the colour of their clothes mutating constantly from one fluorescent shade to another, in time with the music.

'Look at that hyper-trance!' exclaims the girl, pointing at a towering, swirling, iridescent tornado sweeping the room.

'YES!'

'Where are the drugs?'

The pair scan the room.

'Over there,' says the boy.

'Where? Where? I can't see nought.'

'There, there ... Look.'

They set off in haste to the back of the warehouse, where they join the queue of animated revellers.

'What drugs they got?' enquires the girl.

A transperson in a fluctuating, fluorescent-striped outfit

swivels to face her. She/he says in a thick Liverpool accent, 'HyperHyper™, it's amazin' like.'

'What is it?' says the boy.

'An adrenochrome–serotonin blend like,' says the Liverpudlian.

'Let's get some HyperHyper™,' says the boy.

'Go 'ed,' says the Liverpudlian. 'Is right nice one.'

Several minutes later they reach the front of the queue. The girl rushes forward and screams, 'HyperHyper™ adrenochrome–serotonin blend, quick quick!'

'Steady on there young lady,' says the white-coated chemist stationed in front of a 3D printer.

A burly bouncer steps forward. He holds a retina displayer up to the girl's eyes. The chemist inspects her medical and psychiatric reports on a transparent screen.

'Okay, you're fine to go,' says the chemist. 'Which ink do you want? There's a choice of these five.'

The girl prods at the screen and says, 'That one. The fluorescent leopard-print.'

'Okay, that'll be seven credits,' says the chemist.

'Hurry up,' says the boy. 'I can't wait any longer.'

The bouncer with the retina displayer steps towards him.

Forty-five minutes later – As the couple dances tirelessly in time with the hyper-trance, their clothes morph from one fluorescent shade to another, from pink to orange to luminous-green.

'Here it comes, here it comes!' shouts the boy.

'Hold hands with this lot, quick,' says the girl.

The circle of revellers hold hands and watch the towering bands of iridescent colours drawing closer. The breeze becomes a gale when the hyper-trance tornado's swirling, surging sonance descends upon them.

'Here it comes.'

'One, two, three!'

When the hyper-trance tornado hits, the revellers make celebratory whooping noises.

'YES!' says the boy when the tornado has passed.

'Amazing!' says the girl. 'You can actually feel the adrenochrome and serotonin rushing through you in time with the hyper-trance.'

'That was the best experience of my life.'

COFFEE BREAK

AUGUST 9TH, 2084 AD – A COFFEE SHOP – DUKE STREET, LONDON –
37-year-old Terrence has just finished work. He is currently in a
coffee shop, perusing the menu. A waitress approaches. She says,
'Have you decided yet?'

'Yes. I'll go with an organic, environmentally friendly, sustainable
farming, grande Guyanese eco coffee with sanctimonious soya milk.'

The waitress does not depart. She says, 'Before I get your order
I am obliged to give you an overview of coffee farming's history
and warn you of the environmental dangers that irresponsible
coffee cultivation poses.'

'If you must.'

'Traditionally, coffee was cultivated under a shaded canopy of
trees. This provided an important habitat for indigenous free-
living entities. This traditional method did not require chemical
fertilisers ...'

There is a disturbance outside. Terrence, looking out of the
window, sees anti-secularist protesters waving 3D placards and
shouting slogans, denouncing the government's militant secularist
policies.

IRRELIGION

MARCH 3RD, 2085 AD – HEATHROW AIRPORT – ENGLAND – 'Good morning, and welcome to Terminal 3,' greets the Commander.

'Good morning, Commander,' says the new security officer, clicking her heels together at the same time as crossing her arms above her head. 'I vow to protect our secular democracy.'

'As you were. Now, let's get secularising.' The Commander grabs the beret from his desk, plonks it on his head and strides out of the office into the terminal building, the security officer breaking into a trot to keep up with him.

'I am the head of Terminal 3; you'll be reporting to me,' says the Commander, pointing at the insignia on the shoulder of his camouflage fatigues. 'Here on the frontline we need to be vigilant at all times. We are the last line of defence protecting our secular democracy.'

They are passing Tie Rack when the Commander greets the store's manager with an abrupt, 'Morning.'

The manager, holding his arms above his head, says, 'I vow to protect our secular democracy.'

'Cross your arms, you buffoon; it looks like you're surrendering,' says the Commander. 'I'll be popping in later. Need a tie for a secularising ceremony this weekend.'

A group of T-shirt and trainer clad elderly people are coming from the opposite direction. The Commander calls out, 'Where are you visiting from?'

'Miami.'

'Go Dolphins, go Dolphins, go Dolphins!' shouts the Commander, pumping the air with his fist.

The group hurries towards the exit, as fast as their ageing, corpulent legs will carry them.

In comes a flustered-looking man, weighed down by a large bag. Terrence has just returned from a work trip to Brussels.

'Hi there,' greets the Commander. 'Good trip?'

'No, it was tedious. And the queue at passport control is absolutely horrendous. I should be nearly home by now.' Terrence continues on his way.

Above, a swarm of detection bees is being corralled by a bevy of shepherd drones. When the Commander and security officer near the security barrier, the Commander says, 'Stay alert at all times; keep your senses attuned.'

The pair are in the holding pen for UK arrivals, queuing to pass through security. The security officer, surveying the crowded floor, sees the mass of people waiting and hears the relentless whirring of the small, discus-shaped, retina-scanning drones. The Commander lunges towards the queuing people, who emit a collective gasp as they step back. Having grabbed a shrieking woman carrying a baby, the Commander takes a long lingering sniff at her clothes. Turning to the security officer he says, 'You'll get parents grooming children that young. They've been known to hide religious detritus in their bags too.' The Commander claps his hands. 'Now for the tour of the Secularisation Rooms.'

The security officer follows the Commander along the blue-carpeted passageway. To their left is a series of doors. The Commander bursts open the first door. Inside, two bearded, turbaned gentlemen are struggling with the airport security personnel dragging them towards the back of the room, where there are chairs, basins and mirrors. A man with a pair of scissors and an electric razor is waiting beside the basins.

'Stop, we're British citizens!' shouts one of the turbaned men.

'Barber,' says the Commander. 'BAR-BER.' He slams the door shut. The pair continue along the passageway.

An airport security officer is racing towards them. She says, 'Commander, I need your advice. The women I spoke to you about earlier, who were refusing to eat pork.'

'Yes?'

'I tried force-feeding them bacon. But they're refusing to swallow it. Please advise?'

Modern Art

NOVEMBER 30TH, 2086 AD – THE HAYWARD GALLERY – LONDON – Terrence is inspecting a large blackboard covered in unintelligible markings, scrawled in white chalk. A guide approaches. She says, 'You look confused. Let me explain the meaning of this exquisite work.

'Duality is the word that best describes *Modernity Board*. On the one hand, it embodies the frenetic nature of modern life, but it is also a metaphor for childhood, hence the utilisation of a blackboard. Our ancestors during their schooldays used ...'

Terrence is staring at a white canvas. *SPLAT!* The canvas is smeared in what appears to be puke. He spins around and looks for the culprit, but there is no one there. The guide approaches.

'What is going on?' asks Terrence, pointing at the defaced canvas. 'Where did that puke come from?'

'From the Vomitus Expectorator,' says the guide, placing a hand on the contraption beside her, which looks similar to a tennis-ball-serving machine. 'Every ninety seconds it sprays synthetic vomitus, which is then cleaned away in time for it to expectorate again.'

'Why?'

'The artist is representing the innocence and purity of the Earth through the white canvas. The expectorated vomitus embodies the damage we have done to her. Look closely.'

Terrence glances at his watch before leaning forward.

'Note how the vomitus is motley coloured,' continues the guide. 'The green flecks represent toxic waste, the red splatter the deaths we humans have caused.'

'Okay.'

'If you lean forward a little more you can actually smell the vomitus.'

'I'll take your word for it.'

When a girl hurries over and proceeds to wipe the canvas with a mop, Terrence says, 'What have you done to be given this job?'

'I'm here on work experience from the Royal College of Art.' The girl extracts the mop and retreats, just in time.

Terrence walks off. Ahead on the floor is an empty box. Terrence, examining the box, assumes that its empty interior embodies our minds and is supposed to be filled with the viewer's imagination. A gallery employee is approaching. They crush the box with their foot and throw it in a bin. Terrence decides it is time to go home.

FREE SPEECH

OCTOBER 14TH, 2087 AD – A CLASSROOM – STAINES – ENGLAND – 'What is free speech?' Having asked the question, the teacher surveys the class. Commodore is waving his arm in the air. No other hands are raised. At the back of the class, a boy sits with his head lolling to one side, a stream of drool hanging from the corner of his mouth. 'Wake up!'

The boy sits up and wipes his mouth with his sleeve. He says, 'Yeah?'

'What is free speech?'

'Dunno innit.'

Still, Commodore's arm waves.

'How about you?' says the teacher. 'Do you know what free speech is?'

The girl shrugs, says nothing.

'How about you? Any idea what free speech is?'

'Mən başa düşmürəm.'

'I forgot, you haven't learnt English yet.' A boy in the middle row is slowly raising his hand. 'Yes.'

'Free speech is talking that you don't have to pay for, cause it's free.'

'No.' Still, Commodore's hand waves in the air. The teacher sighs and says, 'Enlighten us, Commodore.'

'Free speech is an antiquated practice that most contemporary societies view as reckless and licentious, though it continues to be prevalent in parts of the Americas …'

'The question was, what is free speech?'

34

Consumer Eugenics

DECEMBER 21ST, 2088 AD – A GENE ENHANCEMENT CLINIC – NEW YORK CITY – Walter's blonde-haired wife, addressing the doctor, says, 'He must be blond.'

'Well, that's pretty much a given, honey,' says Walter. 'We're both blond.'

'Your hair is yellow,' says Walter's wife.

'It's blond,' says Walter.

'What do you think, doc?' says the wife.

'Yellow,' says the doctor.

'Blond, yellow, same thing,' says Walter. Neither the doctor nor his wife appears convinced. 'Whatever,' says Walter with a derisory flap of his hand.

The doctor says, 'Would that be a sandy blond, dirty blond, golden blon—?'

'Light blond,' says the wife.

'Eye colour?' enquires the doctor.

'Blue,' says the wife.

When the doctor enters the information on his keypad a hologram of a small child appears.

'AHHH!' shrieks the wife, prodding animatedly in the direction of the child's marginally aquiline proboscis. 'No to that nose!'

'That nose is awesome,' says Walter, running a fingertip along the length of his own aquiline nose. 'It's just like mine.'

'Here we go,' says the wife.

'This nose originates from the nobility from the old country on my grandfather's side, with a dash of Cheyenne from my great-grandmother.'

The wife raises her eyebrows. She says, 'No hooked nose!'

'Not hooked, aquiline,' says Walter.

The doctor looks up at the ceiling, mutters in Spanish, '¡Oh por Dios!' (Oh my God!)

'What's the world coming to?' says Walter. 'My father always taught me that all that was needed for success in life was a zest for being alive and an unflinching belief in free-market capitalism. Nowadays you're telling me you also need a generic nose. Bull-shit!'

'Firstly,' says Walter's wife, 'rhinoplasty has been going on for like forever, okay? Secondly, my kid isn't having your nose, period.'

'You don't want our kid having my noble nose. Fine,' says Walter. 'But in that case, I don't want it having your brain.'

'Why, what's wrong with my brain?'

'Have you got all day?'

'Just because I don't do finance stuff doesn't make me stupid, okay?'

'I never said it did.'

'So, what are you saying, hooked nose?'

'That your brain sucks, that's what.'

'What are you talking about? Give me just one example to back up what you just said.'

'Here's one. Check this out, doc; this is great. You know what she said the other day? That Napoleon was in World War II.'

RUSH HOUR

18:40 – MARCH 10TH, 2089 AD – BAYSWATER ROAD – LONDON – Relentless increases in the price of rail fares finally forced Terrence to abandon the train last year. He now drives to and from work. The rush-hour traffic has ground to a halt entirely. From the deluge of self-drive vehicles comes the sound of remonstrance in the form of beeping. Terrence prods the car horn repeatedly. The car's computer system, concerned by its owner's antics, emits only a few beeps before overruling him. Terrence orders the stereo system to turn on, utters a sarcastic *thank you* when it obeys, then requests the Turn of the Millennium radio station. The sound of the piano-driven ballad *A New Day Has Come* by Celine Dion fills the car. Terrence pounds his fists on the dashboard and demands the stereo system turns itself off, which it does, much to his relief.

The car jolts forward, travels a couple of metres and draws to a halt. Terrence, peering up through the windscreen, sees the omnipresent drones flitting back and forth. An elongated Nile delivery drone looming overhead casts a long shadow on the ground below. Nile drones are so commonplace today that were a young child to be asked what flies in the sky and comes down to land again, they would invariably give the answer Nile drone, not bird.

The car edges forward then stops again. To his left in Kensington Gardens, Terrence observes a group of helmeted Elders following their guide up a large beech tree in spider-like fashion. Terrence, inspecting the scene, is aware from the tree climbers' anachronistic clothing that they were probably born about eighty years ago. Their multi-item outfits, consisting in most instances of a hologram-less top and cargo trousers, are a dead giveaway. Nowadays, most people wear all-in-one jumpsuit-style outfits with either a hologram or picture of the desired outfit on the exterior. With the longest working hours in Europe, few people have the time for multi-item outfits anymore.

The car is moving. Above the road Terrence sees a floating virtual advertising board that reads, *The Last Frontier – let's beat death together – Death Research UK*, underneath which are details for sending donations.

Crossing the road are a group of Christians. They are partaking in a public display of zeal, a common sight since the recent resignation of the short-lived, militant secularist government. They are wearing gas masks, crucifix-engraved cylinders strapped to their backs, rosaries clasped in their hands. The cylinders contain air, but with a lower percentage of oxygen.

A Lenten Gasper collapses to her knees in the middle of the road. Cars jerk to a halt. Terrence is thrust forward in his seat. Leaning out of the window he shouts, 'Get out the road, you pious fu …', the remainder of the remark drowned out by a tirade of car horns.

PIOUSITES

**MARCH 19TH, 2090 AD - CANTERBURY CATHEDRAL - KENT -
ENGLAND -** There is the sound of much lamentation emanating
from the direction of Thomas à Becket's shrine. Gathered by the
shrine are a group of Piousites. Some are crying, others tearing at
their hair.

Not since the Methodist revival of the 18th century has the
Church witnessed such a renaissance. Whilst Methodists believed
that faith produces outward holiness, Piousites are of the opinion
that outward holiness produces faith.

Approaching a cathedral visitor is a shaven-headed Piousite, an
alms bowl clasped in her trembling hands. Having deposited a
couple of sweets into the bowl, the visitor says, 'That's a
remarkable sin-suit you're wearing; mind if I take a gander?'

The sin-suit is emblazoned with holograms of nuclear
warheads, refugee types, hazardous waste and more besides.

An emaciated Piousite elder is sprawled flamboyantly on the
cathedral floor, a withered hand flailing in the air. A woman is
kneeling beside him, examining his apology apparel. Having
pressed her ear to the outfit, she says, 'Wow, you can actually hear
that war orphan wail.' And then, 'Ew, that chemical waste really
smells.'

A cross-bearing Piousite approaches a member of the cathedral
staff and says, '*Sh'lam lek! Mah 'abdah?*'

'Excuse me!'

'Oh, you don't speak Aramaic.'

'I will have stigmata for days!' exclaims another Piousite.

'I wager two Lenten crusts my stigmata last longer than yours.'

SURVEILLANCE SOCIETY

APRIL 4TH, 2091 AD – OXFORD STREET – LONDON – Terrence is returning to CCP headquarters from his lunch break when the disc-shaped retina-reader drone descends and hovers in front of his face.

'Bugger off!' says Terrence, twisting his head away from it and pulling the hood of his raincoat over his face. Terrence has walked but a few metres when he sees a child in a pushchair up ahead holding a hand to its neck, tears pouring down its cheeks.

'Bee sting, bee sting!' it wails.

The mother, bending down, inspects the child's neck. She says, 'That's not a bee sting, sweetie, it's a DNA drone prick.'

THE MAGHREB

DECEMBER 16TH, 2092 AD – THE MIDLANDS – ENGLAND – A boyfriend and girlfriend have just come out of an all-night warehouse rave. They are now travelling in a self-drive car.

'Best party ever,' says the boy.

'Frantic! HyperHyper3™ is the best invention *ever*. It gets you *so* wasted.'

The boy opens the gym bag at his feet and pulls out a six-pack of biodegradable renew beers.

'You've brought the hard stuff,' says the girl.

'Yeah. Let's do it.'

'Freebasing alcohol? That's mental. It's seriously bad for you. And this stuff's really strong – 6%!'

'Do it! Do it!'

'But look at the picture,' says the girl, her mouth turned down at the corners as she inspects the hologram of the pulsating, diseased liver on the biodegradable can in her hand. 'That's just wrong.'

The boy holds his can up. It has a hologram of a man projectile vomiting blood. He says, 'Fuck it, you're only young once.'

He opens the can and takes a gulp. The girl tentatively opens hers and takes a sip, being careful to clasp the can by the rim so as not to touch the pulsating liver hologram.

Twenty minutes later – The girl says, 'Shouldn't we be back in Warwick by now?'

'Yeah,' says the boy, peering out at the winter morning darkness.

'Look, street lights; we must be nearly home.'

'Only it don't look like Warwick.'

'I'm stopping the car,' says the girl. She presses the touchscreen on the dashboard. The car glides to a halt in a parking area. 'Where are we? This ain't home. What d'you enter for the destination when we left the party?'

'Warwick; where d'you think?' says the boy, somewhat defensively.

The girl inspects the touchscreen. Her face turns ashen. She says, 'You dickhead.'

She punches her boyfriend on the arm.

'Ow! What's that for?'

'You didn't enter Warwick.'

'Yeah I did. W-a-'

'You got the wa bit right, yeah. But you put a zed after that, and you must have pressed enter when the results for Waz came up, cause we're in Waziristan.'

'Where's Waziristan?'

'Birmingham.'

'Oh no! Not the Midlands Maghreb.'

'*Yeah.*'

'I'm sorry,' says the boy, struggling to hold back tears.

'Turn the lights off,' says the girl.

The boy complies. He says, 'What do we do now?'

'Wait here till all's quiet and then head home, that's what.' The pair sits sombrely drinking beer, waiting for the road to clear of traffic.

Car lights are scanning the parking area.

'Oh no,' says the girl. 'Get down.'

'What is it?' says the boy.

'Mutaween.'

'The *what?*'

'The mutaween. The religious police.'

'Bollocks!'

'Quick, hide the bevvies.'

Two men are hurrying towards them. They have long beards and are bedecked in camouflage. One of them knocks on the car window.

The boy and girl clamber out of the car.

'We got lost; it ain't our fault,' blurts out the boy.

'کیا آپ یہاں کیا کر رہے ہیں؟'

'You what?' says the girl.

'یہ شراب ہے؟'

'You did good at school,' says the boy. 'You must remember some Arabic from cultural diversity class.'

'He ain't speaking Arabic,' says the girl. 'He's speaking Urdu. Do you know any Urdu?'

'Nought.'

COMPENSATION CULTURE

JANUARY 25TH, 2093 AD – HIGH STREET, BASINGSTOKE – Terrence is on his way home. Terrence wishes he had taken heed of the ominous clouds and taken an umbrella with him. A passing vehicle ploughs through a large puddle, sending a wave of water crashing onto the pavement, soaking his trousers.

'Damn!' says Terrence, who looks left and right before crossing the road. He is in the process of mounting the pavement – one foot placed on it, the other in mid-air – when he slips on the wet surface and falls forward, landing on the pavement on his front. Having picked himself up, Terrence is relieved that he is unharmed, the only sensation of pain being a mild throbbing emanating from his knee. He is poised to continue his journey when he hears a buzzing noise approaching from behind. On spinning around, Terrence finds himself face to face with a compensation-claim hover-hound drone – a small, brown, stumpy-tailed specimen whose plasticine-like apologetic face is dominated by large doleful eyes and a wide mouth curved down at the corners, forming the shape of a crescent moon.

'Fuck off!' says Terrence.

The hover-hound remains where it is, hovering inches from his face. Terrence bunches up his fist and lashes out at it. The hover-hound, having dodged the blow, drifts upwards, out of range of its accoster's now flailing fists.

The drone's eyes open wide and its plasticine-like mouth mutates to form a grin. A speaker on its side proceeds to blare the *Where there's a blame there's a claim* theme tune.

'Shut up!' shouts Terrence, wishing again that he had remembered his umbrella. If he had it with him he might just be able to swipe the hover-hound out of the air and smash it to smithereens with the umbrella's handle.

The music is replaced by the sound of a ringing phone. Terrence is running down the pavement, pursued by the hover-hound, when he hears the heavily accented voice say, 'Thank you for calling Compensation Craze. This is Sanjeep speaking.' Terrence sprints around a corner, darts behind some bins.

Peeking out from between the bins, he sees the hover-hound passing to and fro through the air, its lips forming a horizontal line, eyes raised upwards in an expression of exaggerated perplexity.

'May I start by recording the problematic nature of the accident? *Hello,* sir, I am trying to ascertain the problematic nature of the accident.'

HOME COMFORTS

FEBRUARY 1ST, 2094 AD – 7 CLARENCE CLOSE, WARWICK – ENGLAND – The mother and father have been on an all-night virtual-reality television bender, consisting of *Celebrity Big Brother 2094*. Having taken off his virtual-reality helmet, the father says, 'Wow, did you feel her reaction when she discovered that Ahmed were still in the house?'

'Her heart nearly leapt out of her chest.'

'I could sense it were about to happen. The suspense were incredible.'

'Let's keep goin'.'

'Yeah,' says the husband, rubbing his eyes. 'But I'm absolutely knackered.'

'Print out some more of 'em amphetamines, love. Put the kettle on while you're at it.'

The front door opens. Their son enters the sitting room.

'Mornin',' says the mother.

'Had a good night?' says the father.

'The most brilliant night ever. How was *Celebrity Big Brother*?'

'Fan-tastic,' says the mother.

'A night to remember,' says the father.

When the son joins his parents on the settee, the mother wraps her arm around his. She says to her son, 'Where's your girlfriend?'

'Went home. She's got an interactive soap opera starting at seven.'

'Oh,' says the mother. 'Tell us all about the party. Was it fun? How were the drugs?'

The muscles at the back of her jaw twitch constantly. Bruxism is an amphetamine side effect the pharmaceutical industry is yet to eradicate. The son says, 'The party were absolutely brilliant. We had the best hyper-trance experience ever. The new stuff, the HyperHyper4™'s been perfected. It's like on a timer or someink. The adrenochrome hits yah, then the serotonin blasts your brain in like waves at midnight, exactly.'

'At midnight. Very clever,' says the mother.

'How's it manage that?' says the father.

'HyperHyper4™'s got a timer integrated in it. It's programmed to release the serotonin part at a certain time.'

'Wow,' says the mother. 'But why d'they want to do that?'

'It's so everyone in the party experiences it at the same time,' says the son. 'It means everyone becomes one in perfect harmony. It's called collective consciousness.'

'Oh, that sounds fun,' says the father. 'You didn't end up in the Maghreb again, did yah?'

'Nah, I checked the car's route like ten times before we left.'

'I bet,' says the father.

'I've only got nine fingers nah,' says the son. 'There's no way them mutaween are getting any more of 'em.'

BIBLICAL RE-ENACTMENT

AUGUST 10TH, 2095 AD – STAINES – ENGLAND – The two teenagers had protested vehemently when their parents informed them that they would be holidaying as a family in Bethlehem, via the Staines Virtual-Reality Cultural Centre. The teenagers had been hoping to go on an extreme skateboarding virtual-reality trip. But their parents had been adamant that what the family needed was something educational. No amount of complaining could persuade them otherwise.

On pulling into the Staines Virtual-Reality Cultural Centre car park, the father had commented, 'It don't look like much, does it?'

But any concerns he had have dissipated now, as he lies dormant on his back in his underwear, in the brightly lit, single-person pod, his eyelids fluttering. Like the other holidaymakers, there is a drip attached to his wrist to provide nourishment on the two-day trip. There is also a pipe to remove waste matter.

Having exited the virtual workshop, where they have been learning how to make Aramaic bead jewellery, the parents allow their senses to be immersed by the biblical scene, painstakingly recreated by a team of virtual-reality architects, working in tandem with archaeologists and historians.

The mother is savouring the aromas of unleavened bread, billowing from the stone house on the opposite side of the alleyway. Meanwhile the father listens contentedly to the bleating sheep being driven up the stone path by a shepherd, crook in hand. Here come two Roman centurions in plumed-helmets, the short swords attached to their belts bobbing up and down as they descend the sloped, narrow pathway. When the centurions pass by the parents they say, '*Salve, amandam die ...*'

'Morning,' says the father.

48

'Ignore 'em,' says the mother. 'They ain't welcome here.'

Approaching is a female fellow holidaymaker the parents met earlier in the foyer at the Staines Virtual-Reality Cultural Centre.

'Nice tunic,' says the mother loudly, in order to be heard above the omnipresent bleating of the sheep.

'Oh, isn't it just *lovely?*' says the holidaymaker, looking down approvingly at her multi-coloured robe. Having glanced at her watch, she says, 'Oh, is that the time? I best get going. Got a textiles workshop down Manger Square. See ya later.' She scuttles off down the path, calling back as she goes, 'They've got wool and linen, can be spun rough or fine, so I'm told.'

'We best get goin' too,' says the wife, tugging at the sleeve of her husband's tunic. 'We've got a cultural tour and Old Testament studies to fit in before lunch.'

While descending the path, they gaze at the enormous walls and towers of the fort on Herodium Hill that dominates the skyline. This afternoon they will travel by donkey to the 15-hectare site, where they will enjoy the majestic panorama that extends northwards to the Mount of Olives and eastwards to the Dead Sea. After which they will travel onwards to see Shepherd's Field, where it is widely believed that the birth of Jesus was announced by the angels. This will be followed by a visit to Solomon's Pools. In order to fit all this in, they will utilise the fast-forward feature that allows holidaymakers to get the most out of their days, in addition to alleviating the tedium and discomfort of lengthy trips by donkey. The couple will be back in Bethlehem in time to experience the bustling outdoor market. Physical items cannot be brought back from a virtual-reality trip, but they can be reserved and collected later at the Staines Virtual-Reality Cultural Centre's gift shop.

The couple's teenage children are trudging up the pathway towards their parents.

'Hello, boys,' says the mother. 'You joinin' us for the cultural tour of Bethlehem?'

'Nah,' they say in unison.

'Alright, but make sure you're at Manger Square for eight,' says the mother.

The mother is convinced that Jesus will be making an appearance in Manger Square this evening, and she does not want her children missing out on the opportunity to see him.

One of her children says to their sibling, 'This is *shite.*'

'There's nought to do,' says the other.

A young holidaymaker with a ball held under his arm is tearing down the pathway towards them. On reaching the brothers he says, 'Come doun Lake Galilee and kick a footie abaht.'

'Yeah, alright.'

MALIGNANT MATRIARCH

SEPTEMBER 30TH, 2096 AD – 18B CLAYTON CRESCENT,
BASINGSTOKE – Terrence has just arrived home from a long day at
work. Having set his mug of tea down on the coffee table, he turns
on the holonet with a swish of his hand and then prods at the 3D
pornographic site icon on the favourites bar. A directory
materialises above the table – a mosaic made up of miniature
holograms of porn actresses. Each actress encourages Terrence to
select her, with a beckoning hand, blowing of a kiss, patting of a
derriere, jiggling of breasts or crack of a whip. Terrence opts for a
curvaceous blonde. Having selected the no-holds-barred secretary
scene, Terrence grabs a box of tissues from the table, collapses into
the armchair, undoes his fly and extracts his member from his
pants.

A woman's face appears. She is not the porn star. Terrence
blinks, blinks again. The woman's eyes are fixed reproachfully on
him.

'What the hell?'

'Hello, Terrence.'

'JESUS CHRIST!'

Terrence recoils from the woman and returns his member to
his pants.

The woman opens her wide, censorious mouth. She says, 'Your
pornography consumption is concerning. Pornography is very
bad for you.'

Terrence's face reddens and his pupils dilate.

'Might I suggest some group psychotherapy sessions with other
troubled holonet users?'

'GET OUT OF MY HOUSE!'

'Pornography makes you angry, Terrence.'

'GET THE FUCK OUT!'

Today, Ministerial Matrons, or Malignant Matriarchs as their detractors refer to them, are employed by holonet providers at the state's behest.

Mechanised Maid

OCTOBER 30TH, 2097 AD – 7 CLARENCE CLOSE, WARWICK – The recently purchased mechanised maid, having completed the hoovering, hovers through to the kitchen and deposits the contents of its storage vessel into the bin. It returns to the sitting room, scales the wall and proceeds to polish the ceiling. The homeowner casts a glance in its direction before returning to the dusting of the mantelpiece. The mechanised maid is more than capable of doing the dusting itself, but the homeowner likes to keep a few chores for herself. She finds them cathartic. The homeowner picks up one of the Forever-Frames™ from the mantelpiece, her eyes moist with nostalgia as she views the clip captured in the frame of her then toddler son crawling across the sitting room floor towards the games console. When the child points at the console, the homeowner holds the Forever-Frame™ to her ear to listen to her son's first words. *Play-Stay, Play-Stay ... Play-Stay.* She places the Forever-Frame™ back on the mantelpiece.

An amber light is flashing on a thin, transparent device wrapped to the underside of the homeowner's wrist. She says, 'Mornin.'

A life-sized hologram of her neighbour materialises in the middle of the room.

'Morning,' says the neighbour.

The homeowner, noticing the mug of tea the neighbour is clasping, says, 'Good idea, I'll get a cuppa myself ... Get daun here.'

'You what?'

'Not you, the mechanised maid.'

The mechanised maid stops polishing the ceiling, scales down the wall, hovers across the floor and then waits obediently at its mistress's slippered feet. The homeowner, peering down at the 20-centimetre-high, discus-shaped object, says, 'Cuppa tea.'

The mechanised maid departs in haste. Meanwhile, the homeowner collapses on the settee, the hologram of the neighbour lowering herself down next to her.

'Where are you going for Christmas, love?' enquires the neighbour.

'Polynesia.'

'Oh *lovely*. Is Poly-nesia in Staines?'

'Slaugh.'

A woofing precedes the arrival of a small spaniel, followed in hot pursuit by its canine companion – a robotic dog, of similar size and stature.

'Cruyff, aht!' says the homeowner.

The dog looks imploringly up at her, tongue lolling from its panting mouth. The canine companion, departing the room, swivels its head 180-degrees to face the dog and emits soft woofing noises. When the dog joins its canine companion the homeowner says, 'Good boy.'

Recent legislation requires owners of single dogs to purchase a canine companion. Animal psychiatrists had been arguing for half a century that the absence of one was unethical. Some solitary breeds are exempted.

'Where was I?' says the homeowner, reaching down and taking the mug of tea from the outstretched claw of the mechanised maid.

'You were talking about your Slaugh Polynesia Christmas hols.'

'Oh yeah.' The homeowner takes a sip of tea. 'They're five-star, luxury, single-family huts by the sea. You know, the South Pacific-style ones. The huts've got chimneys built in 'em for Santa.'

'*Oh*, what a good idea.'

'Wake up Christmas mornin' and it's a white Christmas, snow everywhere, all over the beach and that. Great for the nippers to have a white Christmas.'

'What about the grub in Poly-nesia?'

'There's Christmas dinner, all the trimmings.'

'Who's coming?'

'The husband, me, my sister, her two little 'uns and—'

'Two little 'uns? Well I never. You'd have thought one would be more than enough. I dread to imagine how little virtual-reality time your sister must have.'

'It ain't easy, but the mechanised maids help aht where they can.'

'What about your son? He coming to Poly-nesia?'

'Well, he can't come over here in person, but there's a virtual-reality thingy in Vilnius. Uses the same programme, files, whatever you call 'em. We'll all meet up in Polynesia.'

'How's your boy liking it out in Lithuania?'

'He's grateful for the work. There ain't much over here for the young these days.'

'And the mother-in-law – she coming?'

'Nah, she'd never go virtual at Christmas.'

BURNOUT

APRIL 23RD, 2098 AD – COUNTRYWIDE CAR PARKS HEADQUARTERS – PORTMAN SQUARE, LONDON – Terrence nibbles on a fingernail then pulls the hair on the sides of his head. He is in dire need of a break. But what with the forthcoming national rollout of a new car storage stack system, he is too busy. Terrence decides to go to the office kitchen to get a cup of tea. The office does not have a mechanised maid. He scans the office. Directly ahead, two workers toil, their heads bowed over their desks. Over in the far corner Terrence observes the ageing director, reclining back in his chair, conversing loudly on the holophone, his feet resting on his desk. Parked on the floor beside the director's chair is the latest R2D2-style droid.

Having got up, Terrence surreptitiously makes his way across the office floor towards the kitchen. No drinks requests are forthcoming. On entering the kitchen Terrence sighs with relief. After putting the kettle on he stands, leaning against the wall, looking out of the window at the square ten storeys below. Something clangs against the window. Terrence recoils. On creeping back towards the window, he sees the culprit descending towards the road. It is a disc-shaped retina-reader drone. Terrence grits his teeth. Until recently this type of drone performed its irksome duty on crowded, neighbouring Oxford Street. They did not venture here. Having exhaled sharply, Terrence goes over to the boiled kettle and prepares his cup of tea. He adds a soupçon of real milk and one sugar.

'Yo, C-3PO! Dark chocolate truffle mocha.'

Terrence puts his cup of tea down and returns to the hot drinks dispenser. He presses the chocolate truffle mocha option, then selects dark chocolate and the synthetic milk option. When the coffee has been dispensed he walks over to the fridge, takes out the faux cream and squirts it on top of the coffee in a neat twirl. Terrence carries the dark chocolate truffle mocha through to the office. The director is still reclining in his chair, his feet resting on his desk as he converses on the holophone, the R2D2-style droid beside him. Terrence approaches the director, raises the cup up and proceeds to pour the contents over the director's head.

'AHHHH!'

WOOOAH twee-vwoop VRrrUHD DEda dah

CRUCIFIXION

MARCH 16TH, 2099 AD – CANTERBURY CATHEDRAL – KENT – ENGLAND – Situated in the cathedral's northeast transept is a cordoned-off, confession-type booth.

'What happens in the booth?' enquires a cathedral visitor, her question directed to the cassocked female vicar standing beside it.

'A virtual-reality crucifixion experience?'

'Let's give it a go,' says the cathedral visitor to her friend. 'We really must; it's Lent.'

'Not a good idea, darling,' says the friend.

'It will be fine; I can control pain; I've done yoga. Does crucifixion hurt?'

'Yes,' says the vicar. 'Let me explain.' She slides open the booth's door, revealing a tilted crucifix and, encompassing the walls, floor and roof, a television-like screen. There are straps attached to the ends of the crucifix, and pads connected to wires. 'Pain is dispensed through the pads. The pain is superficial but intense.'

'I think you're best sticking to giving up choccy for Lent,' says the crucifixion volunteer's friend.

'No, I can do this. How long is the crucifixion experience, vicar?'

'Five minutes.'

'Oh, that's nothing. If Jesus could do a day, I can do five mins.'

'We'll have to check your medical records,' says the vicar. 'And get you to sign a disclaimer.'

The vicar heads over to the wall and speaks into an intercom. Moments later a church administrator comes scampering. Unbalanced by the Lenten Encumbrance Crucifix around her neck, she trips forward. 'Whoopsee!' The retina displayer she is carrying slips from her hands and slides across the floor. Clambering to her feet, she picks it up and then hurries onwards, drawing to a breathless halt beside the vicar. She says, 'Who is being crucified?'

The administrator scans the crucifixion volunteer's irises, checks her medical records and gets her to press her thumb to the displayer's screen as way of a disclaimer.

'Jump in,' says the vicar, who then fastens the woman to the cross. 'The safety word is Iscariot. Say Iscariot and we'll have you out in a jiffy. All the best.'

Having placed a visor on the woman's head the vicar departs the booth.

'Good luck,' says the friend.

The door slides shut. The cross elevates to a standing position.

'Ow!' shrieks the woman. 'Iscariot ... Iscariot, ISCARIOT!'

The booth door slides open, the cross lowers, the straps are removed. The crucifixion volunteer clambers out of the booth.

'It really, really hurts,' she says. 'Even worse than when I fell over in lacrosse that time.'

'I'm going in,' says her friend.

'No, darling, no.'

The now crucified friend hears the shouts of the crowd and sees their irate, mocking countenances.

'Ow!' she shrieks. 'This really, really hurts.' And then, 'AHHH!'

The pain is far worse than anything she has experienced before. Through her tear-filled eyes she sees the animosity in the faces of the jeering Israelites, the Roman centurions' wry grins, and the mourners too, some on their knees, hands clasped together in praying gestures as they look up at her imploringly. She notices the thieves on the crosses either side of her. The one on her right is behaving pretty admirably, considering the circumstances. The other moans incessantly.

Feeling the blood dripping from the holes in her hands and feet, she wails in agony, but she steadfastly refuses to say *Iscariot*.

Her limp body flops forward. The scene is disintegrating. The booth door slides open.

'Well done!' says the vicar.

GENTLEMEN'S PURSUITS

JUNE 3RD, 2100 AD – MESOPOTAMIA CRICKET GROUND – ETON COLLEGE, BERKSHIRE – ENGLAND – Founded in 1440, Eton College remains to this day one of England's most exclusive schools. Its alumni include royals, authors, actors and numerous prime ministers.

Long ago, Eton had a reputation for being rather insular, but nowadays the school is reaching out to form partnerships with other educational establishments. Last year it formed a partnership with the Hazrat Khadijatul Kubra Boys' Academy & Madrasah in neighbouring Slough, a mere stone's throw away from Eton.

This afternoon a team of first-year Eton boys are playing cricket against their Hazrat Khadijatul Kubra Boys' Academy & Madrasah contemporaries. The game is being played on Eton's famous Mesopotamia cricket field. Conversing amiably on the boundary are the opposing coaches, both prefects in their last year at their respective schools. The Etonian, Eggerton-Smyth (aka Eggi), is wearing a knee-length tailcoat, striped trousers, a white shirt with a winged collar and white bow tie. His contemporary at the Hazrat ... Academy & Madrasah is wearing a throbe (long white robe). On his head is a chequered red and white ghutra (headscarf).

14-year-old Montagu-Bass-Douglas (aka RaRa), his cricket bat clasped under one arm, strides towards the pitch, putting his gloves on as he goes. When he reaches the batting area he adjusts his helmet. Clasping his bat by the tip of its handle with the thumb and index finger of his right hand, he lowers it until it is touching the ground. RaRa bends down on one knee to check that the bat is aligned with the middle stump. He steps forward and adopts a batting position – standing side on, bent forward, bat held firmly in both hands, the head of the bat continuously tapping against the side of his back foot. Some polite applause emanates from the boundary.

Whilst the bowler Makhdoom waits, he rubs the cricket ball against his trousers. He starts his run-up, accelerates on the approach to the bowling crease. The ball spins through the air. RaRa steps forward with his front foot, lashes out with the bat. The ball sails through the gap between his legs and crashes into the centre stump. There is a shout of 'Howzat!'

'Chucky. It was a chucky,' moans RaRa, who is adamant that the bowler used an illegal bent-arm bowling action.

The waiting Etonian batters proceed to complain vehemently to the umpire. They then enter the field of play. A heated exchange with their Hazrat … Boys' Academy & Madrasah contemporaries ensues.

Eggi calls out from the boundary, 'Order, order, return to your stations immediately.'

And beside him the rival prefect shouts, 'لا يشكو ... على المباراة.'

The two teams fall quiet. The umpire orders RaRa off the field. He trudges off, head hung forlornly. When RaRa reaches the boundary, Eggi says, 'Complaining on the field of play is not cricket.'

'But it was a chucky,' says RaRa.

'It was a chucky,' say his teammates.

'Stiff upper lip,' orders Eggi. 'Decorum and sportsmanship are to be exhibited at all times on the field of play.'

THE HOUSE

A QUARTER OF A CENTURY LATER – FEBRUARY 1ST, 2125 AD – THE HOUSE OF COMMONS – WESTMINSTER, LONDON – Stationed on the rows of green benches running either side of the wooden-panelled chamber, are male, female and transgendered ministers. On the right-hand side of the chamber, in the middle of the front row, is the incumbent Prime Minister, Eggerton-Smyth (aka Eggi). Beside him sits his chancellor, Montagu-Bass-Douglas (aka RaRa).

In the rows above, two ministers are having a heated exchange, which now descends into shouting and furious gesticulations. This is a source of amusement for the opposition ministers on the opposite side of the chamber. The Prime Minister calls out, 'Stop bickering. You too, Makhdoom.'

The pair fall silent. The Prime Minister, pointing at a space at the end of the last row of benches, says to one of the bickering ministers, 'Tally-ho, over there in the corner; off you go.'

The minister follows his Prime Minister and fellow alumnus's order. Meanwhile, RaRa converses with Makhdoom, whom he had first become acquainted with on the cricket field all those years ago. Makhdoom is now MP for the Caliphate-on-The-Humber, a semi-autonomous, Tory party affiliated zone in the northeast. The Prime Minister, addressing Makhdoom, says, 'Old bean, we must have a chinwag over a beer … err, ginger beer sometime.'

The Prime Minister scans the rows of crowded benches, searching for a place for the minister. A female minister in the row behind pats the bench beside her and says, 'There's space here.'

Makhdoom whispers in the Prime Minister's ear.

'Oh,' says the Prime Minister. 'You can't have female contact during Ramadan.' He continues scanning the crowded benches.

His attentions fall on a floppy blond-haired minister who is conversing with the minister next to him. When the Prime Minister calls out, 'Monti, Rodi, rehreh!', the two ministers shift along the bench.

CHURCH OF CONSUMERISM

AUGUST 15TH, 2126 AD – A CONSUMERIST CHURCH – NEW YORK
CITY – Stationed in a pew beside his latest wife is Walter. As he
converses loudly with a group several pews in front, he holds his
arm up, exposing his antique watch. Pointing at it with the index
finger of his other hand he exclaims, 'Check out this classic fusion
men's watch! It's a Hu-blot.'

'Hu-blot?'

'Hu-blot are Swiss. This is an antique, circa 2000.'

Someone says, 'What an *antique?*'

'*Antigüedad.*'

'*¡Caray! Qué maravilloso.*' (*Wow! How wonderful.*)

A woman, ogling the watch, says, 'Oh my, that watch looks
really expensive!'

'Damn right, lady, that's cos it is,' says Walter.

'Tell them about the King Gold, darling?' implores Walter's wife.

'King Gold is unique to Hu-blot. King Gold contains 5%
platinum. That's why it's so shiny. Check it out in the light.'

At the front of the church the clergyperson coughs several
times into the microphone. Walter falls silent.

'Let us pray,' says the clergyperson.

Having adopted kneeling positions, the worshippers repeat the
clergyperson's words.

'I now accept prosperity into my life.

I accept abundance into my life

I accept success and materialism

Perfect wealth for my family and future generations

Perfect, overwhelming and abundant wealth in my life

In the name of Jesus

Amen!'

Elixir of Life

OCTOBER 25TH, 2127 AD - THE HOUSE OF COMMONS - WESTMINSTER, LONDON - The Prime Minister, addressing the house, says, 'Our proud nation's track record for invention and innovation is unparalleled. We invented the steam engine, the bowler hat, fly fishing, cricket and driven game-bird shooting.' Drumming his fingers against the table, he tries to think of more inventions, briefly considers adding croquet, but uncertain as to whether the English, he means British, invented the game, decides against it.

'The public–private partnership between my government and Vivere Enterprises,' continues the Prime Minister, 'has led to a medical breakthrough which has resulted in yet another innovation for our nation. I hereby declare that average life expectancy for our nation's citizens is to rise from 119 to 160.' Applause and *here here's* fill the chamber. 'My science minister will now explain the science.'

The science minister steps forward. He says, 'The assault on ageing is to take the form of a three-pronged attack. It entails treatment with a medication derived from the enzyme telomerase, this in addition to parabiotic ageing tissue restoration treatment and stem cell therapy.'

Five minutes later – 'The Hayflick Limit is the number of times a human cell population will divide until cell division stops,' says the science minister. 'Now that we have succeeded in lengthening human telomeres by 1,000 nucleotides, the Hayflick Limit no longer controls us; we control it.'

Ten minutes later – 'Before I explain the effects of the telomerase enzyme-derived medication, might I remind you about what I was saying earlier about telomeres,' says the science minister, oblivious to his yawning, and in several instances snoring, colleagues. 'For vertebrates, the sequence of nucleotides in telomeres is TTAGGG. This sequence is repeated about 2,500 times in humans, give or take. The notable—'

'That's enough,' says the Prime Minister.

'But I-I haven't finished.'

'There's one sure way to bore. Tell it all.'

LIFE EXPECTANCY

MAY 14TH, 2128 AD - 10 DOWNING STREET - LONDON - 'It is imperative that we provide the three-pronged anti-ageing treatments on the NHS Mark II (National Health Service). And that we do so with haste.'

'I beg you to reconsider,' implores the chancellor. 'These treatments are far too expensive to be giving out willy-nilly at no charge. It will be the final nail in the coffin for the NHS Mark II.'

'What do you think?' says the Prime Minister, addressing the only other person in attendance, the health secretary. 'This is, after all, your realm of expertise.'

'I think it is a marvellous idea Prime Minister,' she says. 'The population will show their gratitude come election time.'

'My sentiments exactly.'

'This is insanity,' says the chancellor. 'Our government's legacy, like our predecessors', is supposed to be budget cuts and austerity measures. Not only will this cost a bomb, it is likely to culminate in an increased population.'

'Don't be such a spoilsport,' says the health secretary. 'As for your population concern, I wouldn't worry. What with increased working hours and our obsession with virtual reality, less people are having children these days. The trend is set to continue.'

'I know only rich people are supposed to have good things,' says the Prime Minister, 'but I believe we need to make an exception here. Our ratings are poor, to put it mildly. Offering markedly increased life expectancy is a win-win situation.'

'Eggi, no,' says the chancellor. 'I implore you. We can't afford it.'

'Forget the money side for a second. The population will be in our debt forever. Imagine. Even a lowly refugee might just be able to achieve immortality.'

'Yes, yes, yes,' says the health secretary. 'Can't you see how good it will be for us long term?'

'The hoi polloi,' says the Prime Minister, 'are hoping at best for us to freeze their standard of living. After we offer them extended life, they're not likely to mind too much if we keep taxing the hell out of them whilst going soft on the rich, now, are they?'

'Death is a threat,' says the chancellor, 'but the absence of it even more so.'

'All doom and gloom,' says the health secretary.

'Yes indeed,' says the Prime Minister, who now turns his back on his chancellor and converses with the health secretary.

The chancellor is considering the havoc this extended life policy will have on NHS Mark II budgets, pension plans, potential population increases and the associated housing crisis. The chancellor is feeling unwell. Having retched loudly, he grabs the health minister's designer handbag, turns it upside down, emptying its contents, then turns it the right way up and vomits loudly into it.

'NOO!' screams the health minister.

VANITY

JUNE 1ST, 2129 AD – SWANSEA – WALES – By the middle of the second decade of the new millennium, South Wales had more beauty, tanning and tattoo parlours per square mile than anywhere else in the UK. Little has changed.

Tottering along the pavement in stiletto heels and fluorescent-pink spandex is Rihannalyn and her muscular, fake-tanned, camouflage-spandex-wearing male friend, Bieberyyd. In their right hands they carry gym bags, in their left the current must-have accessory – cosmetic clutches. Cosmetic clutches contain transdermal devices, photo bio-stimulators and therapeutic shockwave tools.

'Tr-aining, hair extensions, sun-tanning pr-oducts, clothes, eyebrow tint*ing*,' says Rihannalyn.

'Teeth whiten*ing*,' says Bieberyyd.

'Your- teeth ar-e alr-eady dazzling white.'

'But I'm r-eally into it. Would not put a pr-ice on it.'

'It's so impor-tant.'

On either side of them are dilapidated houses, interspersed with tattoo parlours and spray-tanning salons. Swansea's tanning aficionados finally figured out that real tanning machines age the skin prematurely and irreversibly.

'Tattoos, tans, fake br-easts, gym member-ships,' says Rihannalyn.

'Diet, clothes, waxing, lip enhancements,' says Bieberyyd.

'Bio-stimulator-s, nails, pageants …'

Looking up at the heavens, Bieberyyd murmurs, 'Don't r-ain, don't r-ain.'

Under normal circumstances this pumped alpha male would not be afraid of rain, but he is running low on fake tan and hairspray, and he has reached the end of his overdraft.

A person passing the pair gives the ubiquitous thumbs-up gesture.

'Br-ill*iant*, that's five Likes since waxing,' says Rihannalyn, stepping off the pavement onto the busy road.

Travelling along the road in his self-drive car is Terrence and his supervisor. They are here for a work conference.

vvvvvVVVVVVVSPLRP!

'AHHHHH!' screams Bieberyyd as his spandex-clad frame is splattered with blood and brains.

The car screeches to a halt.

'Oh no!' says Terrence, struggling to free himself from beneath the emergency airbag.

'You've killed Rihannalyn!'

'It's her fault,' says the supervisor, stepping out of the car. 'This car has the best braking distance in its range.'

Bieberyyd, inspecting his messy spandex, screams, 'AHHH!'

LITTLE ASMARA

SEPTEMBER 3RD, 2130 AD – 7 CLARENCE CLOSE, WARWICK – The mechanised maid is dusting Forever-Frames™ on the mantelpiece. Meanwhile a dog scampers around the room, pursued by its canine companion. Reclining on the settee is the homeowner, a mug of tea clasped in both hands. Beside her a life-size hologram of her friend slurps tea noisily.

'Little Asmara is *lovely*,' says the homeowner.

'Little As what?'

'We locals call Warwick Little Asmara nowadays.'

'Why?' says the friend, who living on the other side of the country is unfamiliar with the term.

'It's mostly Eritreans living here now.'

'Eri who?'

'Eri-treans. Eritrea is a small country in the Horn of Africa. Asmara is its capital.'

'Well I never.'

Having taken a sip of tea, the homeowner says, 'Me and the husband go to the Eritrean market in the town centre every Saturday morning.'

'What they got there, then?'

'Eritrean cuisine amongst other things.'

'Oh yeah! What's Eri-trean cuisine?'

'Eritrean eating habits vary regionally. In the highlands they eat *injera*. Me and the husband love *injera*.'

'What's *injera?*'

'It's a flatbread made from sorghum, wheat or teff.'

'Very *nice*. What else they got?'

'*Hilbet*.'

'Hil what?'

72

'*Hilbet.* It's a paste made out of legumes. Usually fava beans and lentils. And the Eritreans make some lovely craftwork and beads.'

The homeowner picks up a box from the coffee table. It is full of beads. She extracts a red bead and holds it out in front of her friend's hologrammed face.

'*Lovely.*' Frown lines are visible on the friend's forehead when she says, 'If Little As-mara is so amazing, why is it you are thinking of leaving?'

'We are planning to see out our days with other English people.'

'Oh, you're moving to the south of Spain.'

JACKPOT WINNER

OCTOBER 29TH, 2131 AD – HIGH STREET CAFÉ – CHRISTCHURCH, DORSET – ENGLAND – The afternoon-tea rush has just ended and the café's proprietor is clearing up. Following her from table to table is a centenarian customer.

'Nothing good's come out of winning the lottery jackpot,' moans the customer, as she weaves effortlessly between two tables. 'If I'd known what it would be like, I wouldn't have played the lottery twice a week for the best part of a century. Never won a bean. And when I finally did at the beginning of this year, there was nothing I wanted other than top-of-the-range virtual-experiencing equipment.'

'What about all those anti-ageing treatments you've been having?' says the café proprietor, who is presently wiping a table with a J-cloth.

'Oh, don't remind me. I've already spent nearly a million quid on age-reversing cellular treatment thingies. The cost of living these days is scandalous, it really is. If the NHS Mark II had paid for it like we were originally told they were going to, I could have had those anti-ageing thingumajigs for free.'

'You could always stop taking the treatments?'

'Don't be daft! I might very well die of old age if I did that.'

'Why not start doing some activities? You used to enjoy lawn bowls with your friends.'

'Not anymore. They don't want anything to do with me since I won the lottery and started on those cellular treatment thingumajigs. Jealousy, that's what it is. The lottery commercials never warn you about the bad stuff. Mark my words—'

'Sea canoeing? We're right by the sea after all. Or cycling?'

'Never did exercise me, never could see the point of it. Too late to start now at 131 years of age.'

'Travel?'

'No! Can't stand foreign grub, you see. Only English food me.' The customer, looking up at the ceiling, proceeds to list the entirety of her diet. 'Fried breakfasts, roasts, fish fingers, tea and biscuits, trifles, masalas, shepherd's pies, chicken chow meins, summer puddings, stilton, biryanis and samosas. Proper English fare one and all. Can't stand that foreign nosh they eat in other countries.'

'There must be something you like doing?' says the café owner while carrying a towering pile of crockery through to the kitchen.

'Soaps, virtual-reality shows and following celebrities' lives. God knows where I'd be without them celebrities. Don't let anyone tell you getting younger is easy. It isn't. I know. I've already shed half a decade, so the doctor tells me. For all the good it's done—'

'Well, you could always help me clean up here.'

'Oh, is that the time; best get going or I'll be late for *Celebrity Reality Multi-Millionaire*.'

GENDER SHAMBLES

AUGUST 9TH, 2132 AD – A COMMUNITY MEETING – SOMEWHERE –
'I'm sure lots of you have questions. Please, fire away,' says the presenter. Hands are raised. The presenter's attention is drawn to a hand-waving, spikey haired, androgynous-looking individual in the middle rows. The presenter says, 'You ... Yes you, the transperson in the middle.'

'I'm not a transperson. I am a man.'

'Oops, *sorry*. And your question?'

'How long until work is completed—?'

'Nine weeks. The time will fly by, trust me. Next?'

Hands shoot up in the air, including one belonging to a svelte, long-haired person in a dress, stationed near the front. The presenter, pointing at them, says, 'You.'

The person in the adjoining seat to the target points at themselves and says, 'Me.'

'No, not you, the one next to you in the dress. The, um, *woman*.'

'Correct,' says the woman.

'Phew,' says the presenter, wiping his forehead with his sleeve. 'What is your question?'

'When will the facility be upgraded with modern—?'

'By the end of next month at the latest. Next? ... You in the middle in the green. Not you. The one two seats down. The, um, *come on, come on*. I'm going tr-*transperson*.'

'Correct.'

'Get in there,' says the fist-pumping presenter. 'Two in a row; I'm on a roll.'

HUMANOID

NOVEMBER 1ST, 2133 AD – PRIME INN – SWINDON WEST, WILTSHIRE – ENGLAND – With their inhospitable locations, primarily robotic staff and vapid, soulless interiors, Prime Inn is a brand that expounds practicality over hospitality. It is a conference at the nearby Swindon Accountancy Software Centre that has brought Terrence here. It was after his sacking from Countrywide Car Parks back in 2098 for pouring dark chocolate truffle mocha over his boss's head that Terrence made the move to financial software development.

Presently, Terrence is traipsing along the hotel's maroon-carpeted passageway, his companion, a self-drive suitcase, scuttling behind him. The pair stop outside Room 18B. Having pressed his thumb to the fingerprint reader, Terrence enters the room; the suitcase squeezing in behind him narrowly avoids being crushed by the closing door. After parking in an unobtrusive spot by the far wall, the suitcase informs its master as to its whereabouts with a series of beeps.

Terrence, lying on the bed with his eyes closed, listens to the monotonous drone of the self-drive traffic emanating from the neighbouring M4 motorway. Terrence grits his teeth when he considers that at this moment his wealthy, aged American relative Walter is no doubt having far more fun than he.

Rat Race

CITY – 'WOOOO-oooo-OOOOO-WAHHHHH!' 132-year-old
CEO Walter is poised in a crouching position, a tie fastened
around his head, one arm held out in front of him, the other
pressed against his chest, both hands bent forwards 90-degrees.

'Kwa kwa kwa,' utters Walter, jabbing the air with his clenched
fists. And then, 'Kwa kwa kwakwakwakwakwa,' his frenetically
prodding arms a blur of motion. Walter, rotating 180-degrees,
crosses his arms across his chest. 'WAHHH!' A foot flies through
the air at head height, returning gracefully to the floor in the blink
of an eye. 'WOO-ooo-OOO.' Walter adopts the praying mantis
position once more. Meanwhile, the bevy of female employees
perched on his desk emit rapturous applause.

Walter, like so many wealthy people the world over, has
benefitted from the three-pronged assault upon ageing, known
collectively as The Holy Trinity.

A middle-aged junior employee traipses through the office,
greeting his co-workers with desultory *Buenos díases*.

'WAHHHHH. Kwakwakwa. WOOOOO-ooooo-OOOOO!'

No sooner has the middle-aged junior employee sat down than
an amber light flashes on the transparent computer screen on his
desk.

'*Sí.*'

The office manager's severe countenance appears. She says,
'*Limpia los inodoros.*' *(Clean the toilets.)*

In the past when the office's mechanised maid was out of
order, as is now the case, the cleaning of the toilets would have
been given to a young, recent addition to the company. But despite
this employee being in his fifteenth year here, he has been left

78

languishing on the lowest tier, a direct result of the postponed retirement of the company's senior employees. This has prevented the next level of seniority being promoted, which in turn has created a jam all the way down the line.

Giggling is emanating from Walter's office.

'WOOO-ooooo-OOOO WAHHH!'

The middle-aged junior employee sighs, an assistant at the adjoining desk tuts, and on the other side of the office a minion curses.

'WOO-WAH-WOO-WAHHHHH!'

Some of the female employees watching Walter's antics hold manicured hands to their mouths whilst others clap demurely. A young secretary, her svelte frame perched on the corner of Walter's desk, flicks a length of brown hair from her face in coquettish fashion.

Walter brushes the tip of his nose with the index finger of his right hand. This action signifies the commencement of the routine's finale.

'Woo wah WOO WAH WOO WAH WOO WAH WOOO WAHHH!' utters Walter through pursed lips as he bounces around his office on a stockinged-foot, the other kicking the air at a variety of different heights. 'WOO WAH WOO WAH WOO WAH!'

RETIREMENT AGE

18:50 – APRIL 27TH, 2134 AD – VICTORIA, LONDON – Sitting in his self-drive car, peering out at the rush-hour-traffic-strewn road, is 87-year-old Terrence. He has spent over half a century commuting to and from Basingstoke. He has another thirteen years to go until he reaches the mandatory retirement age of 100.

The traffic is still not moving. Terrence orders the stereo system on and then requests the 21st Century Classics station. The sound of *A New Day Has Come* by Celine Dion fills the car. While holding his hands to his ears he demands the BBC News station, then exudes a sigh of relief when on extracting his hands Dion's dismal wails have been replaced by the sound of a news broadcast.

The government has announced today that the retirement age is to be increased with immediate effect from 100 to 110.

'NO!'

II: PLUTOCRACY

FAST FOOD

MAY 21ST, 2135 AD – A FAST-FOOD OUTLET – HOUSTON, TEXAS – AMERICA – A centenarian is waiting in line at the fast-food outlet's 3D printer. Observing a fellow customer selecting her desired items on the printer's touchscreen, she feels a pang of nostalgia on remembering the fast-food outlets of her youth, when more often than not one ordered from a real person. Reminiscing through rose-tinted glasses, she forgets the dehumanising nature of the fast-food industry of yesteryear.

On reaching the front of the queue, she looks up at the illuminated menu above the machine, licking her lips as she surveys the sumptuous array of burgers. Her tongue rapidly retracts when her gaze falls on the milled-mealworm burger option, consisting of a hologram of several large mealworms crawling over a cheeseburger. It was some years back that civic activism finally culminated in fast-food retailers being required by law to offer an eco-friendly alternative to beef. However, the meat lobby insisted that milled-mealworm burgers could only be served on the condition that live mealworms (mealworm beetle larvae) be depicted on the menu alongside the food item.

The centenarian opts for a super-size double beef burger meal with synthetic cheese, then momentarily considers substituting sea algae for lettuce. Having decided against it, she presses the plus button repeatedly to up the carbohydrate level for her fries. Ignoring the red flashing light, she keeps pressing plus until the carbohydrate level is at its max. She selects a large Coca-Cola and goes over to the retina displayer.

The 3D printer churns out the order almost instantaneously. When she grabs the food items the printer says, 'Have a super-duper day!'

The centenarian is surprised that this frivolous farewell is uttered in Olde American, something of a rarity in this increasingly Spanish-language-dominated nation.

An ultra-morbidly obese customer trudges over to the machine, selects a super-size Coca-Cola and waddles up to the retina displayer. The red light flashes and an alarm sounds. No drink is dispensed. Through a speaker in the side of the machine, a voice says, 'You are not authorised to purchase this item. *No está autorizado ... este artículo.*'

'Jeez,' says the customer, who now trudges off.

Today the morbidly and ultra-morbidly obese are not permitted to purchase soft drinks with an excess of 25g of sugar per 300ml.

Do Oneself A Mischief

SEPTEMBER 16TH, 2136 AD – VISIONARIES FINANCIAL SERVICES – NEW YORK CITY – 'WOOOO-oooo-OOOOO-WAHHHHH!' CEO Walter is poised in a crouching position, a tie fastened around his head in customary fashion, one arm held out in front of him, the other pressed against his chest, both hands bent forwards 90-degrees.

'Kwa kwa kwa,' utters Walter, jabbing the air with each hand in turn. And then, 'Kwa kwa kwakwakwakwakwa,' his frenetically prodding arms a blur of motion. Walter, rotating 180-degrees, crosses his arms across his chest. 'WAHHH!' A foot flies through the air at head height, returning gracefully to the floor in the blink of an eye. 'WOO-ooo-OOO.' Walter adopts the praying mantis position once more. The secretary perched on his desk emits rapturous applause.

'WOOOO-oooo-OOOOO-WAHhhhh ahhhh.' Pain surges through Walter's chest. 'Ahhhh!'

'Is everything okay?' says a secretary.

'Ahhhh!'

Walter topples over, crashes into a desk, falls to the floor.

'¡No!' shrieks the secretary.

Faces are peering in from the other side of the transparent wall. No one comes to Walter's aid.

The secretary quickly deduces that her lot might be worse if anything were to happen to Walter. With a slash of a purple-tinted finger she brings up a hologram of the company's management system and locates the contact details for her boss's private health insurance provider.

Convalescence

**THREE DAYS LATER – HELIOPOLIS CARDIAC CENTRE – CAIRO –
EGYPT –** It was his health insurance provider that had him flown
out here to the world's foremost heart transplant clinic. Walter
was close to death when he went into surgery earlier today. He is
presently sleeping on his back, his greyish-hued face surrounded
by a mane of unkempt yellow hair. Walter stirs, his eyelids flutter.
He blinks, blinks again. Everything is blurry. When the blur clears,
his gaze is fixed on a framed picture on the wall at the end of his
bed. It is of an Ancient Egyptian woman with a headdress in the
shape of a throne, a pair of cow horns protruding from it, a sun
disc wedged between them. She is the Ancient Egyptian protective
Goddess Isis. There is a prayer inscribed below the picture. Walter
mutters the words aloud.

'Nehes, nehes, nehes,
Nehes em hotep,
Nehes em neferu …'

BURGERS

APRIL 1ST, 2137 AD – THE WHITE HOUSE – WASHINGTON DC – AMERICA – The President is in his office, working on the draft of a proposed bill, when the holophone rings. He sighs, waves his hand over the holophone and says, '*¿Hola?*'

'What's up, President?'

'Yo,' says the President, instantly recognising the voice of the English-language-preferring, centenarian chairman of the ABI (American Beef Industry). 'Is this urgent? I'm real busy.'

'Sure it is. Now beam me up, Scotty.'

When the President holds his hand over the holophone, a life-sized hologram of the Stetson hat, bolo tie-wearing ABI chairman materialises next to him.

'Howdy partner,' says the ABI chairman, peering over the President's shoulder at the proposed bill. 'Is that anything I should know about?'

'No,' says the President, spinning around in his revolving chair to face the ABI chairman. 'Now, what do you want to see me about?'

'Your campaign trail starts next week!'

'*Sí.*'

'At every stop on the campaign trail, when you get out of your automobile, rotorcraft or whatever it may be, you're goin' to be holdin' a burger. You're goin' to spin around 360-degrees and shout, *¡Me encanta la carne estadounidense!*'

'Shout *I love American beef*. I'm not doing it.'

'I ain't askin'.'

The President swallows.

'On your feet, *boy*!'

The President stands up.

'Now you're goin' to practise. Do you have a burger?'

'Not on me, no.'

'Pretend that antiquated glass paperweight is a burger.' The President picks up the paperweight. 'Hold it out in your right hand. Pretend to take a bite; now spin around.' The ABI chairman does a pirouette and says, '¡Me encanta la carne estadounidense!'

'Are you sure this is a good idea?'

'Sure it is. Now, vamos!'

The President picks up the paperweight and pretends to take a bite from it, spins around 360-degrees and says, '¡Me encanta … estadounidense!'

'Enthusiasm!'

'This is embarrassing,' says the President, collapsing back into his chair.

The hologram of the ABI chairman is looming over the President. He says, 'Do you need remindin' who put you here?'

'No,' says the President, who has not forgotten that the American Beef Industry was instrumental in his campaign to become president.

'We ain't goin' out like the sugar industry. And you're not tramplin' all over us like your predecessors did the Second Amendment. Treating it like it were a piece of trash.'

'And I don't plan to, but—'

'For centuries our proud nation's beef industry has been attacked by tree-huggin' eco traitors with their beef rip-offs: mealworms, synthetic beef and whatnot. Now, let's run through this again.'

CORPORATOCRACY

AUGUST 23RD, 2138 AD – LOWER OMO VALLEY – ETHIOPIA – The NGO (non-governmental organisation) employee was descending towards the landing strip when she saw the enormous holographic banner, stretching across the sky, emblazoned with the message – *Welcome to Tigra Agro Pestari – Environmental, Humanitarian & Palm Oil Enterprise.*

The self-drive jeep kicks up a trail of dust as it races towards the village of Tigra Agro Pestari. Ahead, surrounded by traditional huts, is a towering glass office building, bedecked in Ethiopian and Tigra Agro Pestari flags. The company's flag consists of a bottle of palm oil surrounded by smiling children.

Ethiopian orchestral music plays in the background when the NGO employee ascends in the lift. When she enters the top floor office, the Tigra Agro Pestari director greets her before introducing her to six smartly dressed Ethiopian company employees. The director says, 'Would you like an organic, environmentally friendly, sustainable farming Highlands coffee?'

'Yeah, why not,' says the NGO employee. 'Milk, one sweetener.'

When a male employee gets up to go and get the coffee, the director says, 'Note how it is a man who volunteers. Gender equality is extremely important to us here.'

'Can we get started?'

'Sure, fire away.'

'What is your response to accusations that your company has created a corporatocracy here in the Lower Omo Valley, that your presence is nothing more than neo-colonialism?'

'Ludicrous,' says the director. 'We are in the valley at the behest of this country's government. Our mission is to improve the fertility of the valley and provide training and job opportunities for the local population …'

The director's monologue goes on for quite some time. When he finishes, the NGO employee says, 'And what about the accusation that Ethiopia's President is merely a puppet for the foreign-owned food corporations?'

'Guys, you can answer this,' says the director, addressing the Ethiopian company employees. 'How do you feel about outsiders questioning Edibleoilopia … err … I mean Ethiopia's sovereignty.'

'It is rude!' they respond in unison.

'But the President was formerly an adviser for the foreign food companies based here,' says the NGO employee.

'Cynical people always want to believe the worst. Unfortunately, that's just the way the world is,' says the director. 'And might I add, the President, who I count as a dear friend, is a kind-hearted, generous person and a truly exceptional golfer. If he were in the country at the moment, I'd get him on the holophone to speak with you personally. But it's best we leave him to enjoy his yacht on the French Riviera in peace.'

The NGO employee says, 'Projects like yours have resulted in people displacement—'

'I'm going to have to stop you there,' says the director. 'The term 'people displacement' is illegal in this country. In fact, I shouldn't have just said it.' He chuckles. 'We must respect our host's laws.'

'Well, can you discuss land-grabbing?'

'No, that's an illegal term too.'

'Water depletion?'

'Illegal term.'

'Food security?'

'It surprises me that you've come to someone else's country and haven't read up on the laws of the land. That is a very colonialist attitude, lady! Someone pass our guest a copy of your proud nation's constitution.'

An employee whips out a copy of Ethiopia's Constitution and passes it to the NGO employee. Nearly half of it is dedicated to food libel and defamation laws.

'How about the extinction of the agropastoralist way of life in the valley?' says the NGO employee. 'I can ask about that right?'

'That we can discuss, yes,' says the director. Addressing the employees, he says, 'Give me a yes if you think being a team member of a forward-thinking, environmentally friendly humanitarian company is better than being an agropastoralist?' He points at each employee in turn.

'Yes, yes, yes, yes, yes, yes.'

'Thanks for the coffee,' says the NGO employee. 'I'm leaving. You won't mind if I pop in and have a quick look at your famous palm oil plantation before we go?'

'No can do,' says the director. 'I would be breaking the law if I allowed you to. Of course, if it were up to me ...'

They are heading towards the lift when the director says, 'I tell you what I can offer you. That's a trip up the valley to visit a Saudi Arabian rice fiefdom. The Saudis have been part of the fabric here since the early 2000s. Great guys, and girls! Really progressive lot the Saudis. They put the beheading and rampant migrant worker abuse behind them decades ago.'

'I'm not going to a Saudi rice fiefdom.'

'Fine, suit yourself.'

They get in the lift. Peering down through the glass exterior, the NGO employee sees locals in tribal dress preparing for a fancy-dress parade, to be put on in her honour.

PIONEER'S PRIDE

MAY 26TH, 2139 AD – THE WHITE HOUSE – WASHINGTON DC – The President is in his office memorising a speech when the holophone rings. Pressing his palms together in a praying gesture, he mutters, *'Por favor, no el director de ABI.'* Having waved his hand over the holophone, he says, *'¿Hola?'*

'Good morning President.'

'What's up?' says the President, relieved that it is the Canadian-born chairwoman of poultry behemoth Pioneer's Pride, and not the American Beef Industry chairman. 'Do you want me to beam you up?'

'Nah, voice only.'

'How's living in Virginia treating you?'

'Fine; you know, no different from anywhere else when it comes down to it.'

'Have you been doing much golf?'

'Eh?'

'Have you been doing much golf?' repeats the President.

'Being chairwoman of the largest chicken producer in America and Puerto Rico, and the second largest in Mexico, doesn't leave much time for golf.'

'I can certainly appreciate that. Now, how can I be of service this fine day?'

'You are going to change South Carolina's name to Pioneer's Pride.'

'I must have misheard. I thought you said—'

'You are going to change South Carolina's name to Pioneer's Pride.'

'Are you out of your goddamned mind?'

'There are 6.84 chickens for every person in this country. Have been since the second decade of this millennium,' says the chairwoman. 'Pioneer's Pride owns 90% of those chickens. Within the next ten years it will be 100%.'

'Don't do this, please,' implores the President. 'South Carolina is the home of the ... Carolina Hurricanes hockey team. You Canucks love hockey.'

'Those rink rats can keep their name; it's the state we're after.'

'This is sacrilege, blasphemy ... heresy!'

'Branding trumps all those things.'

'GODDAMN IT!'

'Pioneer's Pride is South Carolina's economy. We move our operations elsewhere, or go robotic, what's going to happen to the poorest state not named Mississippi? A state with nothing to lose is a dangerous state.'

'The American people will never allow this to happen.'

'They've got no say in the matter.'

BANKER'S BONUS

JANUARY 13TH, 2140 AD – CITY OF LONDON – ENGLAND – Behind the mahogany desk sits the bank's grinning chairman. Addressing the banker opposite him, he says, 'Your performance has been first rate once again this year. Your £40m annual bonus is fully merited.'

The banker, sitting impassively, says nothing.

'In addition to the bonus,' continues the chairman, 'your dedication has earned you the right to join the most exclusive order known to humanity. It is with great pleasure that I announce that you are to forthwith commence the necessary procedures required for membership of the guild of Vitam Aeternam. I hereby grant you the gift of potential eternal life.'

'YES!'

Boreout

FEBRUARY 5TH, 2141 AD – FSD ALL STARS HEAD OFFICE – VICTORIA, LONDON – 94-year-old financial software developer Terrence is at his desk. On the other side of the office, the managing director is drinking from a mug emblazoned with the words, *Don't Fear, Financial Software Is Here!* Every year at the Annual National Financial Software Conference the managing director gets a new slogan-inscribed mug. The mugs are stored in chronological order on shelves above the managing director's desk.

Looking across the office at the shelves, Terrence retraces the mugs until he locates the last one whose slogan had made him chuckle. He finds it fifteen mugs from the end. Its slogan – *I'm an FSD not an STD!* After that, humour had given way to the banal and the downright depressing. Terrence starts reading the slogans for the years that followed.

I ♥ Financial Software
Superstar Software, Software Superstar
Coffee ++
Coffee + Financial Reporting = My Life

The managing director, mug in hand, approaches Terrence's desk. She says, 'Is the system advisor model CT10Q level 2b report ready?'

Terrence nods; the managing director walks away. When Terrence says, 'Instructing Printer FS1X,' a green light appears on the printer behind him. 'Print report CT10Q 2b. Three copies, one-sided, A5, full-spectrum colour, ultra-eco paper, white.'

Language

JULY 18TH, 2142 AD – LEBANON, SMITH COUNTY, KANSAS – AMERICA – The ABI chairman is in his garage, doing some work on his Eco SUV. Sitting on the bonnet of the vehicle watching him is his great-nephew. The ABI chairman says, 'Pass me the spanner boy.'

'What is a spanner?'

'You know what a spanner is! It's right there, on the bench in front of you.'

Having slid off the bonnet, the great-nephew inspects the array of tools on the bench. He says, 'Which is the spanner?'

The ABI chairman strides over to the bench, picks up the spanner and says, 'This is a spanner. You must know what a spanner is.'

'You mean a *llave inglesa?*'

'*Llave inglesa* is Spanish American. We speak Olde American. It's a spanner. You tellin' me you never heard of a spanner?'

'Never heard of no spanner.'

The ABI chairman goes over to the garage entrance, leans out and shouts, 'Niece!'

When his niece and great-nephew's mother enter the garage, the ABI chairman says, 'Your boy don't know what a spanner is.'

'Why would he? They're called *llaves inglesas*, have been for years. Logan Cerrone, you are a livin' fossil!'

HOFFERS

FEBRUARY 14TH, 2143 AD – MALIBU BEACH – LOS ANGELES COUNTY – AMERICA – A procession of tanned males with immaculately coiffured hair are jogging along the sand. They are wearing matching red shorts. Each carries a red life float in their right hand.

Followers of the Hoffer sect often congregate here on this hallowed ground, where the 1990s show *Baywatch* was filmed.

POLITICAL ADVERTISING

AUGUST 17TH, 2144 AD – AN OLDE AMERICAN LANGUAGE BROADCAST – THE WHITE HOUSE – WASHINGTON DC – 'It is my firm belief that the Healthcare Reconciliation Act XXXVI will prove to be beneficial for all,' says the President. 'I would now like to reiterate to my fellow Americans what I outlined earlier today in Spanish American.

'This act has been passed with the aim of increasing affordability and quality of health insurance ... First and foremost, this act will reduce the cost of healthcare for you, the people. Before I continue I have an announcement to make. A dozen foot-long turkey dawgs are now only $20 at Walmart, SuperValu Inc., Grupo Comercial Chedraui, and Grupo Gigante. That's right, tasty, foot-long turkey dawgs, only $20 for a dozen at all participating stores. So, hurry on down and get your tasty foot-long turkey dawgs while stocks last. Gobble, gobble, gobble, yum, yum, YUM!

'And now back to the Healthcare Reconciliation Act XXXVI ...'

CRYOGENICS

SEPTEMBER 29TH, 2145 AD – VISIONARIES FINANCIAL SERVICES – NEW YORK CITY – Walter discharges a deep 'WOOO-ooooo-OOOO' sound as he crouches, one arm held out in front of him, the other pressed against his chest, both hands bent forwards 90-degrees. He springs to his feet and proceeds to hop across the floor on one foot, the other kicking the air frenetically at head height, first one way then the other, the movement a blur of motion. 'Kwa kwa kwakwakwa.' The two secretaries clap enthusiastically when Walter hops back in the direction from whence he came. 'Kwa kwa kwakwakwa …'

A grinning Walter grasps the ankle of a giggling secretary. He says, 'Your turn.' Having lifted her leg up he says, 'Now twist your hip over girl.'

The secretary emits a playful shriek and then squeals, 'No, no, it *difícil*.'

Walter releases the foot. Turning his pink telomerase-treated face to the other secretary, he says, 'Your turn missy.' The holophone starts ringing. When Walter answers the call, he says, 'Yo!'

'*Disculpe que lo moleste.*' (*Sorry to bother you.*)

'How many times I have to tell yah? Olde American.'

'*Perdón*, err … I mean sorry,' says the junior, middle-aged employee who is sitting on the opposite side of the transparent divide from Walter's private office.

'What's up?'

'The New Brunswick Freezing Hall's on the line.'

'Put 'em through.'

Walter signals for the secretaries to leave the office, with a flap of his hand.

''Ello, Mr Van Dyk, dzis is zhe CEO of zhe New Berunswick Fereezing Hall.'

'What's up, Frenchie?'

'I am phon*ing* regard*ing* you*er* wife, Mrs Van Dyk.'

'Corvette, yeah. What of her?'

'Do you wi*sh* to beam m*e* over so w*e* can conv*er*se face to face?'

'I'll give it a go.' Walter passes his hand over the holophone. A hologram of the female New Brunswick Freezing Hall CEO materialises next to him. Walter says, 'Nah, we're doing this old skool.' When he swipes his hand over the holophone the CEO disappears. 'Now, what's up?'

'When you*er* wife Mrs Van Dyk perished, w*e* were hop*eful* zhat it was on*ly* temporar*y*.'

'Go on,' says Walter, now ogling a secretary's pert posterior on the other side of the transparent office wall.

'I have good news! When you*er* dear wife's cognit*ive* abilities declined, scientist*s* were aware zhat it was not du*e* to cell death or neuron*al* loss. After all, zhis was not Alzheimer's, but som*ething* *euh* complex and sinis*ter*. Zhey knew it was du*e* to alteration*s* in zhe neur*ons'* morpholog*y*. However, zhey were not sure how to restore zhe dendritic spines of zhe cortical pyramidal neur*ons* and dendritic arb*ours—*'

'Get on with it lady, I ain't got all day!'

'Well, there is now a cure. You*er* wife is ready to retur*n* to life.'

'Ah!'

'As zhe next of ki*n* we need your consen*t*. Zhen we'll have her resurrected by zhe end of zhis mon*th*.'

'Keep her on ice!'

'*Euh*. For how *long?*'

'Get back to me in a century. Bye.'

CHICKENS™

JUNE 13TH, 2146 AD – PIONEER'S PRIDE (FORMERLY SOUTH CAROLINA) – AMERICA – The elderly farmer gulps when he sees the black truck racing along the farm track towards him, a sibilating drone following in its wake. Having lowered the pails of water to the ground, he thrusts his trembling hands in to the pockets of his faded denim overalls. The truck slides to a halt, sending clucking farm fowl scattering in all directions. The doors swing open and three burly, camouflage-clad men jump out, each weighed down by a piece of military hardware that looks like it has come straight out of an early 21st-century shoot-'em-up computer game. A fourth man gets out of the vehicle. He is wearing an all-in-one black suit and wrap-around sunglasses. Ignoring the farmer's welcome of, 'Hey, y'all,' he says to the three men, '*Espera aquí ... con este old coot.*' He then strides up to the farmer and says, 'Howdy redneck.'

'Great day in de mornin',' says the farmer, who is poised to elaborate, when the visitor, pointing at a feathered fowl pecking in the dry grass, says, 'What the hell is that two-legged, feathered monstrosity?'

The farmer follows the direction of the visitor's finger, looks at the feathered fowl for a second and exclaims, 'Dat's a chickin!'

'That ain't no chicken™.'

'Two leg-s, feather-s, beak, and it a-cluckin'. Dat's a chickin!'

'The head look awful similar to a chicken™, I'll warrant you that. But a chicken™ is a four-legged, featherless beast.'

'You gotta be kidd'n' me.'

'Does it look like I'm kidd'n'?' says the visitor, gesturing with one hand at the three heavily armed men leaning against the vehicle, atop of which rests the drone. When he whistles, the

101

drone takes off and flies over. 'The patent for chickens™ is held by Pioneer's Pride, the largest chicken™ producer in America and Puerto Rico and the second largest in Mexico.'

'God darn!' says the farmer, who now stands gawping at the black drone hovering a metre or so above his head.

With its tail and blades, it resembles a miniature helicopter, only its front is comprised of a flat screen.

'This is Bernie,' says the visitor. 'Bernie's a patent-protector drone. You are now in patent violation.'

'Dang!'

The drone swoops down and proceeds to follow a startled feathered fowl who, clucking noisily, dashes across the sun-scorched grass. The farmer, prodding animatedly in the direction of the fleeing feathered fowl, says, 'I ain't aggervatin'. I don't 'ave no edgy-cation, but I got smarts. Dat dere's a chickin.'

'Stop your hollerin'. Now, the evidence Bernie is recording is being fed live to Carlson & Cortez Co., the lawyers representing Pioneer's Pride here in Pioneer's Pride (formerly South Carolina).'

'Sumbitch!'

'We've been informed you've been sellin' these feathered fiends of yours to folks, claiming they are chickens™.'

'It jes bidnis. I been gallivatin' ever where; I ain't kickin' up no ruckus but I et and I eet dem chickins …'

'Stop squallin', start listenin'. BERNIE!' The drone stops its pursuit of the feathered fowl, flies over and lowers itself to head height. Spanish writing appears on its screen. 'Olde American, *por favor* Bernie.' The writing transforms into English. 'Now, you listin' here redneck.' The visitor proceeds to read from the drone's screen. 'This Pioneer's Pride Chicken™ Production Agreement (hereinafter "chicken™ Production Agreement" or "Agreement") is made and entered into by and between PIONEER'S PRIDE CORPORATION (hereinafter called the "Company") and the "Independent Grower".

WHEREAS, Company is engaged in, among other things, the growing and processing of chickens™,

WHEREAS it is necessary that such chickens™ be raised in conditions to comply with applicable regulations.'

The farmer shakes his head. He says, 'Sump'n outta kilter. Dis carry on's mighty confusin?'

The feathered fowls pecking in the grass cast constant concerned glances in the direction of the drone.

'Chickens™ are to be kept in 500ft by 44ft houses, supplied by the Company,' continues the visitor. '25,000 chickens™ to a house, no more, no less. The loan for that house is to be secured from the Bank of The Carolinas. Do you understand me, boy?'

'Hell no!'

'I wouldn't be callin' a horse a hawg. And you better not be callin' those feathered fiends of yours chickens™?'

'What de I call em de-n?'

'Feathered fowls, farm fowls, feathered fiends, fowl fiends. Anythin' but chickens™. And don't call 'em eggers™ either, or broilers™, or *pollos*™ for that matter.'

The farmer's mouth is hanging slackly open.

'The judge don't like patent infringers, and he don't like patent imposters, or patent interferers neither. I find out you've been gallavantin' around town callin' your fowl fiends chickens™, me and my *hombres* here will drag you to the judge. Did I mention the judge used to be a lawyer for Pioneer's Pride?'

The farmer gulps when he looks over at the heavily armed men leaning on the vehicle.

'Now, you wanna dispute this in a court of law, it'll cost you $5,000,000 to take Pioneer's Pride to trial. And that sum only get you to the table. You ain't even started rollin' yet.'

'Sumbitch!'

The visitor strides over to the vehicle and holds his hand out underneath the drone. Out of a slit at the bottom of it, an A4-sized document emerges. He grabs the document, strides up to the farmer's front door, peels off the back of it and slams the sticky side to the door. The notice has *Violación* printed at the top in a big, red font. Having returned to the vehicle he says, '*Vamos.*' The men get into the vehicle and close the doors. And then the truck is racing off down the farm track, the drone following in its wake.

CYBERWARE

JULY 11TH, 2147 AD – HOLBORN, LONDON – ENGLAND – Terrence's cousin is a street cleaning operative employed by a private company. When the London Borough of Camden gave his employer the contract, a stipulation was that one in three cleaning operatives must be human.

Terrence's cousin is ambling along the pavement. He is holding the handle of his cylindrical self-vacuuming unit with one hand, a leaf/rubbish grabber in the other. On his back he carries a bin. Two of his colleagues are passing along the pavement in the opposite direction. When they sense the close proximity of their co-worker, a row of blue lights flashes across their fronts. He acknowledges their greeting by raising his leaf/rubbish grabber.

His 1.03 metres-tall cylindrical colleagues are equipped with integrated leaf/rubbish grabbers and paving polishers. Their names are R31-D31 and R34-D34. Terrence's cousin picks up a biodegradable drinking vessel with his grabber and drops it into the bin on his back, at the same time as easing his self-vacuuming unit from left to right with a dexterous twist of his wrist.

Up ahead, a group of lawyers have just left work. Unannounced, they start doing backflips in unison along the pavement, over and over again, like a troupe of circus monkeys.

'Tossers!' mutters Terrence's cousin.

Today it is not uncommon for prestigious employers to provide matching cyberware upgrades for their employees. In this instance, flexible spinal disc implants. The given employer's motivation is that the uniform upgrade encourages camaraderie, bonding the team and providing for no end of fun. In this instance the back-flipping upgrade is also a misguided attempt to reinforce the law firm's slogan: *We bend over backwards for our clients.*

As if on cue, a group of lawyers come hurrying out of the law firm on the opposite side of the road, adopt handstand positions and proceed to race along the pavement on their hands at great speed.

'Wankers!'

Terrence's cousin's employer does not provide cyberware.

Regenerative Medicine

NOVEMBER 23RD, 2148 AD – LEBANON, SMITH COUNTY, KANSAS – AMERICA – The aged ABI chairman has been throwing American footballs to his great-grandnephew all morning. He is now indoors talking to his niece.

'My shoulder's still tinglin' when I throw the ball long. I swear it is,' he says. 'That regenerative shoulder surgery cost more than the Eco Warrior out there,' he adds, gesturing with a nod of his head in the direction of the SUV on the other side of the window. 'The surgeon keeps tellin' me it's all in my mind. A psychological trick, he says, a muscle memory of when I had that shoulder trouble. I ain't buyin' it!'

'Stop your squawkin'. You're 150 years old and still throwin' balls all mornin' long. Most folks at 150, they already in the ground, or close to it. They sure ain't throwin' no balls no more. You remember that slogan we used to see and hear way back on those health insurance commercials? *La salud es mejor que la riqueza.* Health is better than wealth. Well, you've got both!'

'What a stupid slogan it was. There's no health without wealth. Not when you get to my age anyhow.'

REBELLION

DECEMBER 5TH, 2149 AD – A MEETING HALL – NEW YORK CITY –
The meeting hall is filling rapidly, its interior a cacophony of
eager, anticipatory voices, which descend into screams and
obscenities when a surveillance drone swoops through the door
and proceeds to dart around the hall, sibilating shrilly. An
attendee, having grabbed an antiquated broom from a cupboard,
clambers onto someone's shoulders and lashes out at the drone.
With a swoosh the drone flees the hall, its departure met by
rapturous applause. Attentions turn to the speaker, who is
standing on a podium at the front of the hall facing their
followers. The followers chant, *'¡Líder de la Juventud! ¡Líder de la
Juventud!' (Youth[1] Leader!)*. One of those chanting is the middle-
aged male junior employee from Walter's firm.

---

[1] In the 22nd century, 'youth' (Spanish: juventud) is a label attached
to anyone below 70 who feels/is perceived to be disenfranchised.

PLUTOCRATS

THE SAME EVENING – WEST POTOMAC PARK – WASHINGTON DC –
A bevy of Renaissance Men (male centenarian fraternity) are
gathering on the grass.

'Buenas noches, bitches,' greets the short trousers and trainer-
wearing, biodegradable can of Bud Super Light-clasping
centenarian. Having driven the blade of his penknife through the
base of the can, he holds the opening to his mouth before spitting
out the beer and exclaiming, 'WOOOW!'

He joins the circle of Renaissance Men observing their
fraternity's leader, the sinewy, yellow-haired Walter, who is
performing a kung fu routine on the grass.

'WAHHHHH. Kwa kwa kwakwakwa. WOOOOO-ooooo-
OOOOO!'

Walter, who recently postponed his retirement indefinitely, is
celebrating his 149th birthday. All week the members of his
branch of the Renaissance Men have been celebrating the event.
This evening's frolics will commence in customary fashion with
the usual theatrics – foot races, muscle-flexing, handstands, tugs
of war and showing off holograms of their latest conquests on
their mobile holophones. When a sprightly 107-year-old arrives,
he high fives his companions.

The members gulp from their cans of Bud Super Light and
chatter animatedly whilst watching Walter hopping around on one
leg. 'WOO-WAH-WOO-WAH-WOO-WAHHH!'

Once the Renaissance Men have concluded their theatrics here,
they will be exercising their Second Amendment rights (curtailed
from centuries past) in a suburban gun club. After which they will
be heading to a strip bar. The Renaissance Men will not be
associating with their female equivalents, Renaissance Women. As

is the case with most other age-defying societies the world over, Renaissance Men and Renaissance Women rarely socialise. Both genders find something deeply unsettling about witnessing the antics of the age-defying members of the opposite sex.

The sprightly 107-year-old late arrival jumps up and down whilst gulping greedily from a can of Bud Super Light. Having dropped the empty can to the ground, he is off, tearing through the park. Though short and squat in stature, anti-ageing treatments, in addition to new hips, knees, ankles, lungs and heart, enable his limbs to pump with much fervour. Emitting celebratory whooping noises, he sprints ever faster. Diving forward, he somersaults through the air, landing on his coccyx. Not even the pain diminishes his euphoria. These emotions of glee complement the permanent expression of joy sculpted on the tightly drawn features of his anti-ageing-treated countenance. Unlike many of his fellow frats he never experienced the joys of youth the first time around. Obesity had seen to that.

Walter, hearing the celebratory whooping noises in the distance, pauses a kick mid-air. He glances upwards, clicks his fingers. The two disc-shaped security drones hovering above the treeline tilt to face their master. Walter holds a finger aloft and gestures with his other hand in the direction of the exuberant 107-year-old. A row of flashing green lights precedes the departure of one of the drones.

Until recently Walter would never have considered employing security drones, but that all changed on a visit to a shopping mall. Walter, clad in silk kung fu pants and a T-shirt with the words *You're Only Young Twice* emblazoned across it, had been scampering through the mall when an outstretched leg had tripped him over, sending him sliding across the floor on his stomach, the little bags from the *parfumerie* and *chocolatier*, containing gifts for his girlfriends, falling from his grasp. Having clambered to his feet, Walter had adopted a defensive white-crane stance – standing on one foot, the knee of the raised leg held at waist height, arms stretched out horizontally at his sides. Scanning the crowd of shoppers for the assailant, he had noticed for the first time resentment: resentment directed at him.

MEMORIES

MARCH 21ST, 2150 AD – LEBANON, SMITH COUNTY, KANSAS – The ABI chairman is having lunch with family members when his great-grandniece asks him, '*¿Crees en Dios?*' (*Do you believe in God?*). And then he is accosted by his other great-grandnieces, all-asking, '*¿Crees en Dios?*' at the same time in their little high-pitched voices.

'Olde American,' says the ABI chairman. 'How many times I have to tell yah all?'

A great-grandniece says, 'Do you believe in God?'

'Sure I do. I saw him one time. It was the spring of '38, 2038 that is. April 5th to be exact. Scientists and those weather folks been warnin' for quite some time that real big tornados were on their way. Global warming and what not, they were claimin', had somethin' to do with the severity of what they were expectin'.

'In them days I was livin' on a farm, ten miles north of here, direction of Red Cloud. Ten miles bein' sixteen kilometers in today's measure. It was late mornin'. I was in my SUV headin' home from town. Sky was fillin' up with black cloud and the wind were a howlin' somethin' awful. Then I saw it, tearin' across the prairie that tornado was, right toward my property. Tore the whole damn thing right off into the sky it did. Took my wife, both daughters and a mighty fine German pointer along with it. The tornado came spinnin' right past me. That's when I saw him. Engraved in the grey spiral was the bearded, grinnin' face of God. Towerin' up all the way to the heavens he was. One big, ugly biblical badass!'

CENTENARIAN GAMES

JUNE 15TH, 2151 AD – CENTENARIAN GAMES – ATHENS – GREECE – Whilst athletes from the Caribbean, particularly Jamaica, remain a dominant force in international sprinting, they are conspicuous by their absence in the older age groups. Centenarian sprinting events are comprised for the most part of Monegasque moguls, Swiss bankers, German honchos, Bruneian royalty, affluent Americans, Nigerian notables and Chinese chiefs. With regards the long-distance events, Ethiopians, Kenyans and Eritreans might be the men, women and trans people to beat at the younger age groups, but they do not have the stamina to go head to head with Italian fashion-brand owners in the centenarian steeplechase, let alone keep up with Indian industrialists in the centenarian half marathon.

The first double centenarian athletics event in history is about to take place. The sense of excitement in the stands is palpable when the German hedge-fund manager turned 100-metre hurdler shakes out her aged limbs before taking up position in the starting block. There are no other athletes competing. Though an increasing number of people are living to see 200, this is the first still-competing athlete to do so. Poised in her starting block in the searing heat, she focuses on the challenge that lies ahead, in the form of ten hurdles, each a height of 83.8 centimetres (2.75 feet).

Even stationary as she is now, the double centenarian athlete gives the impression that she is moving with great haste, so tightly drawn are her pink, telomerase-treated features, her mouth so stretched it is fixed in a permanent grimace. The translucent skin hanging around her neck and knees belies the honed muscles rapidly twitching beneath. She puts her excellent health down to sauerkraut and parabiotic tissue restoration treatments.

The starting gun firing sees her shooting out of the block and tearing towards the first hurdle, which she reaches in seven strides. She leaps effortlessly over with the grace of a gazelle, to rapturous applause from the audience. Keeping a smooth three-stride pattern between the hurdles and a flawless jumping technique, she is cruising towards the finish when her back foot collides with the hurdle mid-air. A gasp from the crowd as she stumbles forward, her arms waving at her sides. Somehow she retains her balance and crosses the finish line. Having seized a German flag and a bouquet of flowers from event staff, she races along the perimeter of the track.

'*Ich bin unaufhaltbar!*' (*I am unstoppable!*) she shouts when she sees her time of 12.47 seconds appear on the electronic board. And then leaping high in the air, '*Ich bin einfach der beste!*' (*I am simply the best!*)

If this were a standard international athletics event, the organisers would be disturbed by her frenzied appearance – bulging eyes, twitching muscle fibres and drooling mouth. So disturbed, in fact, that she would be escorted straight to a drugs test. But in the Centenarian Games, drugs are a prerequisite for any athlete not wishing to compete in a casket on wheels.

The American Dream

FEBRUARY 27TH, 2152 AD – A MEETING HALL – WASHINGTON DC – Virtually every walk of life is represented by the assembled youthful (late teens-eighties) males, females and trans people. They chant, '*¡Revolución! ¡Revolución! ¡Revolución!*'

When the people finally stop chanting, one of the revolutionary leaders says, but in Spanish American, 'Before we think about revolution, we need a plan.'

'What we are proposing is social democracy,' says another leader, also in Spanish American. 'As many of you probably already know, social democracy is a political ideology with a commitment to representative democracy. Social democracy supports intervention, be it social or economic, for the purposes of promoting social justice. And it does so within the framework of a capitalist economy.'

A woman at the back of the hall shouts out in Olde American, 'Social democracy ain't nothing new. All you're doing is regurgitating President Roosevelt's New Deal.'

Someone shouts, 'Speak Spanish American lady.'

'Fuck you! I'll speak my own language in my own country.'

Much shouting ensues. A leader bangs her fist on a table, says, 'Speak the language you choose. We will translate everything anyway.'

Only the Olde American will be provided henceforth.

Someone says, 'We were talking about this new idea, social democracy.'

'It ain't nothin' new! There was a social democratic dude from the Democrat Party early this millennium.'

'Well, it isn't that easy coming up with original ideas,' says one of the leaders.

'The principle of social democracy might not be new, but it's good, real good in fact,' says someone. 'The divide between rich and poor in our country has been growing bigger since the 1960s.'

'And the middle class has been under siege for centuries. Is the middle class's destiny to go the way of the passenger pigeon?'

A man calls out, 'Who are the middle class?'

'They're supposed to be us, I think, but they don't really exist anymore,' calls out someone. 'Nowadays there are only plutocrats, celebrities and the rest of us!'

'What are passenger pigeons?'

'It was a type of pigeon once endemic to the North American continent that was driven to extinction at the start of the 20th century.'

A woman near the back of the hall stands up and says, 'What's this democratic socialism thang ya'll talkin' about?'

'NO!' says one of the leaders. 'We're proposing social democracy. You said democratic socialism. Democratic socialism was democratic control of a socialist economic system. Our system, social democracy, entails creating the conditions within a capitalist system for greater egalitarianism and democracy.'

The sound of applause fills the hall. When the applause has died down, one of the leaders says, 'Who here has heard of the American Fantasy?'

'Course we have,' reply the audience. 'Everyone's heard of the American Fantasy.'

'Who has heard of the American Dream?'

The room is silent.

PLUTONOMY

APRIL 9TH, 2153 AD - A SPACESHIP - SPACE - The returning astronauts are peering down at Earth. One says, 'You can see everything – the oceans, mountain ranges, the Great Wall of China.' And then, pointing at a speck of green in the middle of South America, 'Look, the Amazon Rainforest.'

'Yes. Plutonomy looks like paradise from up here.'

PHARAOH

06:45 – JUNE 23RD, 2154 AD – SOHO, MANHATTAN, NEW YORK CITY –
'WAHHH!' shouts 152-year-old Walter as he leaps out of bed. In
the bed his two wives sit up abruptly. 'WOOOO-oooo-OOOO-
WAHHHH!' Walter's foot sails through the air 180-degrees at
head height before returning to the floor. The wives lie back down
and pull the sheets over their heads. 'WOO-ooo-OOO!' Walter
races off in the direction of his dressing room. Like the rest of this
top-floor luxury penthouse, the dressing room is bedecked in
Ancient Egyptian-themed finery. There are giant vases, genuine
framed papyrus scrolls hanging from the walls and wardrobes
brimming with gold-trimmed tunics and pharaoh-inspired
headdresses. A fusion of reed flutes, harps, rattles and
tambourines play constantly in the background. Today, Walter is
office bound, so he goes with an all-in-one silk suit and shiny
black kung fu-style shoes.

He is now jogging down the penthouse's panoramic, pyramid
mural-plastered passageway, on one side of which are paintings of
Ancient Egyptian gods that stretch from floor to ceiling. There is
the lioness-headed Sekhmet, the jackal-headed god of embalming
Anubis, and the falcon-headed Horus. Walter stops when he
reaches the protective goddess Isis and mutters his daily prayer.

'Nehes, nehes, nehes,
Nehes em hotep,
Nehes em neferu …'
(Awake, awake, awake,
Awake in peace
Awake in beauty …)

It was eighteen years ago, during Walter's convalescence in the
Egyptian capital after heart transplant surgery, that he had an

epiphany, resulting in his conversion to the religion of the Ancient Egyptians.

Walter is now in the penthouse's primary bathroom, perched on a pharaoh-style throne, brushing his shoulder-length yellow mane, at the same time as inspecting his tightly drawn pink telomerase-treated features in the mirror. This expansive bathroom, the penthouse's *pièce de résistance*, is the envy of Walter's associates. It has been painstakingly created to be a microcosm of a stretch of the Nile in northern Middle Egypt, around 1280 BC. The room is in a constant state of flux. Not only does the time here correspond with Egypt's, so do the seasons. It is 06:57 in New York City, but here in the bathroom it is 13:57. On the wall to Walter's right, a barge rowed by slaves drifts slowly past under a hot sun. In the foreground by the near bank, ducks quack contentedly in the shade of a cluster of papyrus.

In the centre of the room lies an enormous sunken Egyptian marble bath. To lie in the bath is to be a floating reed, for the floor of the bathroom is an exact imitation of the glistening tidal waters of the great river. When the tide flows towards the sea the bather is given the impression that they are drifting north, allowing for spectacular views of the necropolis of Beni Hasan to their right on the east bank, followed shortly thereafter by the pyramids of Lisht and Dahshur to the west. At the change of the tides the bath swivels around and the bather has the sensation that they are travelling in the opposite direction. This is achieved through a series of complex optical illusions and by the utilisation of retractable bathroom units, which stay out of sight behind the walls when not required. High above the bath, on the ceiling's imitation sky, there is an outline of the ankh – the key of the Nile, or *crux ansata* (Latin for cross with a handle). The ankh is the ancient Egyptian hieroglyphic character that reads *eternal life*. After dark it appears as a star constellation, illuminating the night sky.

Sunset finds the bathroom at its most magical. The

penthouse's occupants will often congregate here to marvel at the yellow sun casting a red light, silhouetting the pyramids in the background, the sky teeming with clamorous Egyptian geese, spoonbills, ibises and marbled teal heading to their roosts. It is said that there is no finer sight in all Manhattan.

A Nile perch surfacing sends ripples coursing across the floor's shimmering surface. But Walter has no time for the joys of the river this morning. Having completed his coiffure, he swallows his anti-ageing and tissue-preserver pills, then inserts his age-defying eye drops before gargling his restorative mouthwash. He leaves the bathroom. Two of Walter's young children are racing down the corridor, pursued by a maid wrapped in a white cloth.

'Good morning *Faraón* Walter,' greets the maid.

'What's up Nubian?'

Walter, continuing along the passageway, passes a cat-headed mechanised maid coming in the opposite direction. A white loincloth-clad butler is standing by the entrance to the penthouse's escalator. He is holding out a platter draped in a white napkin, on top of which is a ceramic drinking vessel.

'Good morning, *Faraón* Walter,' greets the butler.

'Yo,' says Walter, who now grabs the drinking vessel and downs its contents – caffeinated spirulina (blue-green algae). Having returned the vessel to the platter he bounds up the escalator, strides past the aquatic feature complete with real ibises and then prods a button on the haunches of one of the roof's pair of colossal stone sphinxes. The sphinx splits down the middle, revealing a top-of-the-range plutocraft. Moments later Walter is airborne. Only a select group of senior plutocrats and celebrities are permitted to use personal flying machines, for the air above the city is reserved for the most part for delivery drones. Below the plutocraft, the roads heaving with rush-hour traffic, is a scene identical to centuries past. At the corner of Ann Street and Broadway a group of anti-plutocrat protesters is gathered. When Walter swoops down low over their heads, the crowd shake their placards at him and scream insults. On climbing upwards, he slams his fist against the dashboard and roars with laughter. Every day anti-plutocrat protesters converge here in the Financial District, and every day Walter incurs their wrath in this manner.

Walter is preparing to land on the roof of the towering high-security Wall Street office block that serves as the headquarters of his new company, Renenutet, named after the Egyptian goddess of wealth.

EMOTICONS

AUGUST 7TH, 2155 AD – C SCORTUM & CO. – CITY OF LONDON – Two of the private bank's directors are inspecting a printout of a job application.

C Scortum & Co.
20 Cock Lane
The City of London
London

Dear C Scortum & Co.,

I am writing to express my interest in the position of account manager at C Scortum & Co. It would be LOL to be a part of such a prestigious and iconic bank.

My eight years of banking experience have been GR8 😊. After graduating from university, I spent three years at an investment company, followed by five years working as a bank manager and investment adviser ⎯😊⎯.

Please find my completed application form attached. I look forward to hearing from you 😊.

L8R

Francesca Rodriguez 😊

One of the bank directors says, 'I find her emoticons rather crass.'
'Blasé!' says the other director.

'Take her first emoticon. The grin. It is excessive. A hint of a smile would have sufficed.'

'Quite.'

'And then there's this, ⸺😃⸺. Whilst lauding one's achievements is necessary, the sheer width of it is boastful.'

From outside comes the sound of shouting. The directors look out of the window. Below on the street anti-plutocrat protestors are on the march.

DOGMAS

DECEMBER 1ST, 2156 AD – ELEVEN MADISON PARK – NEW YORK CITY – Walter and his fellow plutocrat are dining here at Eleven Madison Park, one of the city's oldest and most exclusive restaurants. Walter is presently inspecting the menu. Meanwhile, his dining companion eyes the gold, broad-layered collar worn around his fellow plutocrat's neck.

'What is that thing around neck, Walt?'

'A 24-carat-gold weskhet.'

'Wesk what?'

'Weskhet,' says Walter. 'Ancient Egyptian pharaohs and noblemen wore 'em. They're awesome.'

'You really are getting into Ancient Egyptian stuff, aren't yah? Or is it just for show?'

'Hell no, it's not for show. I follow the Ancient Egyptian religion.'

The plutocrat guffaws. He says, 'You can't be serious. Following the religion of the Ancient Egyptians; that's absurd.'

'Absurd, huh? What about you? You have a religion?'

'Hoffer.'

ANTI-AGEING

JULY 19TH, 2157 AD – RENENUTET HEADQUARTERS – FINANCIAL DISTRICT, MANHATTAN, NEW YORK CITY – Playing on the foyer's holovision is Fox News. Experiencing it is coffee-sipping CEO Walter. When the broadcast cuts to a sea of chanting anti-plutocrat protesters, Walter mutters, 'Jealous buttholes.'

An office employee is approaching. She says, 'Boss, one of your *inglés* ... err, English *familiares* is on the holophone.'

It better not be that dildo Terrence. Having selected the holophone's sound-only option, Walter says, 'Yo.'

'Hello Walter,' says the English female relative.

'What's up?'

The relative, wary of getting straight to the point, decides to commence proceedings with some small talk.

'How are things in the Big Apple?' And then, 'Did you get to experience any of the World Cup football?'

'If you mean the soccer, yeah I did.'

'Soccer, hehe. You mean football?'

'I mean soccer.'

'Come on, Walter, it's called football. After all, we invented the game.'

'What's invention without innovation?'

'Cut us some slack Walter, please. We nearly won the World Cup.'

'Nearly. What's nearly? English for an ass-whooping?'

The relative laughs and says, 'I love your sense of humour. Only the other day I was telling my friends how amazing you are and—'

'What do you want?'

'I just err ... wanted to say um ... how grateful I was when you sent over those anti-ageing bacterium boosters last Christmas. It is virtually impossible for normal people like myself to source decent anti-ageing products over here these days. And the prices are so extortionate. I imagine anti-ageing bacterium boosters are no big deal for highly successful geniuses like you. But I appreciated them so much.'

'And?'

'Um ... is there err ... any chance you could send me some more? I mean I wouldn't ask if I didn't really need them. I would be so indebted to you if you could.'

'Nah.'

'Walter, please, I am beseeching you. Have some mercy.'

'No way.'

'PLEASE!'

'SCORE YOUR OWN SHIT!'

THE CONSTITUTION

SEPTEMBER 17TH, 2158 AD - WASHINGTON DC - The executive committee of the burgeoning social democratic movement is meeting in this basement, barely five minutes as the drone flies from the White House.

'Our once-effective capitalist system was the envy of the world at one time. That's what I heard anyway,' says a committee member, but in Spanish American. 'At any rate it isn't no more. Today the age-defying plutocratic elite have a vice-like grip on the nation's government. We are now living in an apartheid system.'

'Tell us something we don't know.'

'Okay, so what do we want to change?'

There is a flurry of responses, in Spanish American and Olde American.

'Replace tax relief for plutocrats with a super tax!'

'No corporate welfare.'

'And no more deregulation of Wall Street.'

'A compulsory retirement age, and a legal age limit too.'

This is followed by *yeahs*, whoops and applause.

'We must have euthanasia laws. The aged must make way for the young.'

There are more whoops and applause. Someone says, 'Let's discourage celebrity worship.'

'*Hello*, we can't do away with traditional values. Celebrianity is part of our culture.'

'Yeah, that's a bad idea. The free exercise of religion is enshrined in the First Amendment.'

Someone saying, 'No more Second Amendment curtailments,' is met with applause. 'Enough is enough, I wanna keep my air rifle.'

More applause and whooping. One of the executive committee members says, 'Any more suggestions?'

'Make America great again!'

'Let's stay clear of vague, dumb-ass slogans. That one's been used before anyhow, loads of times.'

'Yeah, Reagan said that.'

'And that dude with the fucked-up hair.'

Someone shouts, 'They're our islands!'

'Damn right!' respond the committee members.

'China has no rightful claim to Hawaii. They are not disputed islands.'

'Yeah,' concur the committee members, 'they're ours.'

A woman says, ''Em Chinese can stay down in South America in their own country.'

'China isn't in South America. You sound like a latter-day Sarah Palin.'

'Sarah who?'

'Never heard of her.'

'Who was she?'

'It don't matter.'

'Keep the suggestions coming.'

'Tuition-free colleges and universities.'

'An end to the housing crisis.'

'No more Second Amendment curtailments.'

'We've had that one already.'

'Prison time for plutocrats profiting from illegal fossil fuels,' says someone at the back. 'Hell, they did it to us for hundreds of years for selling drugs, and they're candy compared to that shit.'

There is applause and cheering too. When it begins to subside, a member says, 'Excess should be restricted to the virtual-reality realm, and frugality encouraged for reality. This is the only way we can save the planet dudes. Rampant consumerism must stop!'

'You mean consumerism isn't the only way?'

Someone says, 'I've got this cool idea, guys. It's like the best idea ever.'

'Well, go on.'

'Instead of having a senate that represents corporations, let's have a senate that represents us, the people.'

'YEAH!'

'I love that idea.'

'Awesome! That's the best idea I ever heard.'

PRESIDENT SUIT

OCTOBER 11TH, 2159 AD – HOLOVISION STUDIO – LOS ANGELES – AMERICA – Slumped in a chair in his underwear is the President. A bevy of assistants are fretting over him – applying makeup, combing his hair, and so forth. An animated assistant says, *'¿Dónde está el traje del presidente?' (Where is the President Suit?)*

Multiple pairs of eyes scour the room. Someone is pointing in the direction of some clothes hangers hanging from a rail. The assistant hurries over to the rail and extracts an all-in-one business suit, shirt and tie. Plastered across the suit are logos – a fast-food chain brand name wraps around the front, a mortgage provider's emblem embellishes the shoulders, a pharmacy chain's tagline runs down the arms, and on the fronts of the top part's pockets are depictions of air rifle pellets, the words *Ammo Depot* printed beneath.

The Formula One-style business-cum-boiler suit is unzipped and the President steps into it. A member of the holovision station's production staff appears from behind a curtain. She says, *'Presidente, es hora.' (President, it's time.)*

Revolución

APRIL 19TH, 2160 AD – RENENUTET HEADQUARTERS – FINANCIAL DISTRICT, MANHATTAN, NEW YORK CITY – Having landed the plutocraft on the roof of his high-rise Wall Street office block, Walter descends to the top floor, bursts open the door and emits a 'WAHHH!' as he does a jumping two-footed kung fu kick through the air.

An aged plutocrat emerging from a personal oxygen capsule says, 'Mornin' Walt!'

Another, leaning back in his chair, wipes his nose with his sleeve and says, 'WOW! This HGH (Human Growth Hormone) is grade A gear. Want a line, Walt?'

'Nah, I mainline that shit.'

A portly junior plutocrat, throwing back his head, downs a shot of super-spirulina sea algae. Having slammed the shot glass on his desk, he says, 'What's up Walt?'

The three plutocrats, all company directors, gather at Walter's desk and start talking shop.

On the lower floors where the junior wage slaves toil, Spanish is the dominant language, but up here on the top floor these aged plutocrats converse in the language of their birth.

'The Bahamians are refusing our reduced offer for their banana crop,' says the portly plutocrat, pouring himself another shot of super-spirulina sea algae.

He is poised to continue when the HGH-sniffing plutocrat, pointing out of the window in the direction of the street far below, says, 'Never seen so many!'

The other plutocrats look out of the window. The whole street is crammed with tens of thousands of placard-waving protesters.

'Anarchist ass wipes,' says Walter.

'Pussies.'

'Terrorists.'

'We've got security up the ass,' says the portly plutocrat. 'They can't get in, can they?'

When the plutocrats return to their conversation, one of them gestures at a shaded blue area on the West Coast of a holographic map of North and Central America. He says, 'The blue area is where the Bahamians can conceivably transport their bananas for a price better than we're offering.'

'Nothing goes through the Panama Canal without my say-so,' says Walter.

'That's the West Coast out,' says the HGH sniffer as he racks up another line.

'Well, Walt,' says the portly plutocrat, 'what's the Bahamian banana plan?'

'Put the squeeze on 'em.'

Twenty minutes later – Walter cups his hand to his ear when he hears the commotion many floors below. He orders the portly junior plutocrat to head downstairs and find out what is going on. The remaining plutocrats continue talking shop. From several floors below, they hear the portly plutocrat scream, 'COMMIES!'

The trio, now peering out of the window, see protesters pouring into the building.

'Oh fuck!' says one, his pinkish telomerase-treated face instantly paling. He retreats to the back of the room, where he huddles by the exit to the roof with his colleague. Meanwhile, Walter adopts a defensive white-crane stance – standing on one foot, the knee of the raised leg held at waist height, arms stretched out horizontally at his sides.

'Woooo-oooo!'

Moments later the portly plutocrat scrambles into the room, collapses on the floor and says breathlessly, 'There's err ... a traitor; they err ... let 'em in.'

From far below comes the sound of thousands of feet racing up the escalators. When 159-year-old Walter spins around and bounds across the room, he does so with the speed of an NFL running back. Then he is out through the exit, up the stairs and onto the roof, his fellow plutocrats in hot pursuit. Walter clambers into his plutocraft, two plutocrats into the back. There is no room for the portly junior plutocraftless plutocrat.

'PLEASE!' he implores as he dangles from the rail on the bottom of the plutocraft. Walter reaches out with a kung fu shoe-clad foot and stamps down on the portly plutocrat's hand. 'NOOO!' screams the portly plutocrat on the descent.

And there he lies, looking up at his American Dream disappearing into the sky. From below comes his new reality in the form of thousands of stampeding revolutionaries.

The three plutocrats look down at the hordes of protesters pouring through the Financial District, chanting, '¡Revolución! ¡Revolución!'

Walter steers towards his apartment block in the SoHo area of Manhattan. Littered across the sky are hastily erected holographic screens, broadcasting simpering revolution-praising celebrities. These celebrities are banking on the populace's worship of celebrity exonerating them. The flying plutocrats are acutely aware that this is an avenue not afforded to them, for they know how reviled they are amongst their own people.

FALL OF THE BULL

FIVE HOURS LATER - BOWLING GREEN PARK - FINANCIAL DISTRICT, MANHATTAN, NEW YORK CITY - Tens of thousands of revolutionaries have gathered here at the famous Charging Bull. Also known as the Wall Street Bull and Bund Bull, the 3,200-kilogram, 3.4 metres (11 feet) tall bronze sculpture has been a mascot for Wall Street since its installation in 1989. Or rather it was. To chants of *Libertad* and *Revolución* the Charging Bull was toppled onto its side a couple of hours back. Hordes of revolutionaries are now jumping up and down on its carcass, cheering and whooping. A drone is circling above the protesters. From its speakers it repeatedly blares, '*Aléjese, por favor*'. It then repeats the request in Olde American. 'Move back, please.'

The protesters reluctantly clamber off the bull. Through the throng of revolutionaries comes a person with a laser cutter. To loud cheers the person approaches the bull and crouches down by its genitalia, the same genitalia that for centuries have been rubbed for good luck and prosperity by visiting tourists and superstitious business people alike. When the laser cutter severs the bull's genitalia, the crowd shouts, '*¡LIBERTAD!*' The revolutionaries proceed to hug each other, jump up and down and emit celebratory whooping noises. A revolutionary says to a comrade, 'What happens now?'

'Well, I guess that's about it, unless David Hasselhoff's going to turn up and sing *Looking for Freedom*.'

ON THE RUN

THE NEXT DAY - PANAMA - CENTRAL AMERICA - 'Kwa kwa kwakwakwa,' utters Walter as he bounces around in the heat, jabbing at the cloud of flies with his fists and feet. He has stopped here, in plutocratic-friendly Panama, to refuel, prior to continuing on to South America. 'WOOOO-oooo ...!'

One of the plutocrats who flew down here with Walter calls out, 'Walt, I've finally got the President on the phone.'

'About time.' Walter grabs the thumb-sized transparent mobile holophone, sticks it to the underside of his wrist and then holds it to his mouth. He says, 'Yo, President.'

'*¿Quién es?*'

'Walter.'

'*¿Quién?*'

'Walter Van Dyk. President of Renaissance Men twice, chairman of the 0.1 Per Cent Club four years running, winner of the 120-plus national wushu tournament three years in a row. That's who!'

'*¿Quién?*'

'THE BOSS OF RENENUTET!'

'*¡Sí! El tipo—*'

'Speak Olde American.'

'You're the dude with that bathroom, right?'

'What's my bathroom got to do with anything?'

'How did you get my number?'

'From the ABI chairman.'

'AHHH!' shrieks the President at the mention of the aged chairman of the ABI (American Beef Industry).

'Now beam me up, Scotty!' orders Walter.

But the President, who has no desire to be faced with a hologram of the ageing plutocrat, says, 'No, I don't think so.'

'No? You want me to come up there and whoop ass?'

'After all the recent upheaval I need to relax. I am on my way to the golf course. What is it you want?'

'Golf! There's a goddamned revolution going down and you're playing golf. For chrissakes! Drive those commies out before they take Washington DC like they did New York City yesterday. What the hell are the military doing? Kwa kwa!'

'I am resigning as president, in order that a new democratic socialist government can be put in place.'

'You're crazy. Your legacy will be the first president to resign since whatever his name was. Is that what you want? Now, get those commies out, you hear me?'

'They're not commies. They are normal people who don't want the rich taking everything for themselves.'

'WAHHH!'

'How can the young have any opportunity for prosperity and success when 200-year-old immortalist plutocrats like yourself are keeping everything—'

'Hey, who you calling 200 years old? I'm 159. Now listen. State economic intervention will kill the country, jackass. Do your job and get them out.'

'My job,' says the President, 'consists of hawking burgers for the ABI chairman one day, turkey dogs for someone else the next. I can't take it anymore. I refuse to be a plutocrat lapdog—'

'America is supposed to be the land of opportunity. All us plutocrats are doing is living the American Dream.'

'No, you're living the American Wet Dream.'

WINE TASTING

THREE MONTHS LATER – A WINE TASTING EVENT – OXSHOTT, SURREY – ENGLAND – Terrence raises the wine[2] glass to his lips and takes a sip. He nods in approval, mutters, 'Not bad.'

On the opposite side of the table the event organiser, having taken a sip from her glass, says, 'Note the delicately fragrant flavour.' The attendees sitting either side of her raise wine glasses to their lips and take tentative sips, their eyes rolling upwards as the taste diffuses through their mouths. 'Well, do you concur?'

The drinkers nod and mutter in agreement. Terrence sees the event organiser scowl when someone says to the person sitting next to them, 'The recent events in America are quite extraordinary. One can only imagine what will happen here. My personal opinion—'

'We are here to discuss wine,' intrudes the course organiser. 'Now, close your eyes and surrender yourself to your olfactory receptors.'

The mention of events in America turns Terrence's thoughts to his American relative. News has reached Terrence that Walter is on the run. Terrence is picturing his aquiline-nosed nemesis being brought to justice. Observing Terrence's beaming countenance, the event organiser says, 'Is there something amusing you want to share with the rest of us?'

Terrence shakes his head, has a sip of wine. Approaching the adjoining table is a tail-coated waiter. He is clasping a bottle of wine, its base cushioned in a white napkin. The waiter is poised to introduce the wine, when one of the attendees, seeing that it is a Tasmanian Cabernet Sauvignon, dismisses him with a derisory

---

[2] Wine has a lower alcohol content than in centuries past.

flap of a hand. A second waiter appears, brandishing a bottle of Finnish Pinot Noir. When the same attendee signifies his approval, the waiter proceeds to pour the wine.

At another table Terrence hears someone say, 'Now, tilt the Chardonnay. Observe if there is any difference in colour at the rim.'

Someone says, 'It's lighter than the 2139 Norwegian Sauvignon Blanc we just tried. That was a lemon green, this is pale gold.'

At another table Terrence hears someone exclaim, 'Enough of this New World tripe! Waiter, bring me a 2137 Icelandic Merlot.'

Terrence has had quite enough of this facetious nonsense. When he gets up and walks off, he ponders that what with the escalating political situation many of these attendees will soon have more to worry about than the origin of their wine.

NAVY SEALS

THE SAME DAY – ARGENTINA – On board the rotorcraft is a Navy SEAL platoon consisting of sixteen heavily armed SEALs. Far below them the waters of the Río de la Plata give way to the sprawling city of Buenos Aires. Minutes from now they will begin their descent to the landing pad, where a waiting amphibious vehicle will transport them to their target, a notorious former Wall Street plutocrat by the name of Walter, who is hiding under an assumed identity in the northern suburbs. His host of charges includes derivative deceit, environmental sabotage, weapons profiteering and the subjugation of the poor, both domestically and abroad.

The commander of the platoon finishes outlining the forthcoming mission with the Spanish word for alive – *'Vivo!'*

The SEALs respond in unison with the eternal war cry of the American Navy. 'HOOYAH!'

Pop Culture

THE NEXT DAY – THE BREAKFAST ROOM – 10 DOWNING STREET – LONDON – The Prime Minister and his chancellor are taking their afternoon tea.

'Just because there has been a revolution in America does not necessarily mean there will be a revolution here,' says the Prime Minister. 'You are beginning to sound as paranoid as your predecessor.'

'Prime Minister, can you not hear the demonstrators?'

The Prime Minister, having placed his porcelain teacup on its saucer, cups a hand to his ear. He says, 'Yes, I can hear some distant commotion. It's probably merely a handful of dissenters letting off steam.'

'If there's been a revolution in America, there will be one here, mark my words. We always copy America.'

'No we do not.'

'Yes, we do.'

'You have examples to back up your preposterous claim?'

'Burgers,' says the chancellor.

'And reality television.'

'UFC.'

'Crack cocaine.'

'Hot dogs.'

'Garbage Pail Kids.'

'What are Garbage Pail Kids?'

'They were 1980s humorous, satirical trading cards,' says the Prime Minister. 'We have one of Europe's finest private collections in the family. Remind me to show you them sometime.'

'Cupcakes.'

'Cupcakes, yes! But there are also numerous examples of American culture that we did not copy.'

'Like what?'

'Spanish.'

'Okay, and?'

'Baseball, rampant gun crime, turkey dogs and drinking hats.'

'Drinking hats?'

'A drinking hat is a hat with a drink and drinking straw fastened to it. I can count on the fingers of one hand how many drinking hats I have seen on these shores.'

The door opens and the Prime Minister's butler enters the room. When the butler refills the chancellor's cup with tea, she says, 'Lovely tea, by the way; what is it?'

'Ceylon Sonata.'

'Do we have any more of that cake left from yesterday?' says the Prime Minister.

'No, I'm afraid not, Prime Minister,' says the butler. 'It was a little stale this morning, so I fed it to Woof Woof.'

'Very well.'

The butler leaves the room.

'My concern,' says the chancellor, 'is that the people are demanding the dissolution of the government. They are going to force it upon us through a revolution, I fear.'

'Well, they will just have to wait until the general election. Those are the rules of engagement. To do otherwise would not be cricket.'

'The problem is there's a bigger gap between rich and poor today than for centuries. The people feel that there is no legal way to change the status quo. They are demanding that the system be demolished and rebuilt.'

'It's all good and well them saying that. But we mustn't forget that we are a democratic government, and as such do not answer to the people but to the banks.'

LUXEMBURGISM

TWO DAYS LATER – HYDE PARK – LONDON – ENGLAND – Over three hundred thousand demonstrators are gathered here in Hyde Park. Terrence is here. Standing on a podium in the middle of the park is the Revolutionary Socialist leader. This is not your typical political party leader. She/he sports a red and black Mohawk hairstyle, nose ring and military fatigues.

'Whoever you vote for, the corporations win!' states she/he.

Terrence hears someone say, 'That's so true; I'm definitely voting for her/him.'

'For centuries the government propaganda machine has told us that capitalism is democracy. This is a lie,' continues the revolutionary leader.

Above the crowd a murder of crowd-funded bright-red revolutionary drones is descending upon a government democratiser drone that flees the park, displaying its contempt for the proceedings with furious beeps.

'Only through social revolution can society be rebuilt, for how can the apple be saved when the core is rotten?' continues the leader. 'Today is the dawn of a new age!'

There is applause and cheering. Someone standing by Terrence says, 'Check out the hologram of Che Guevara's face shimmering in the sunlight on her/his's combat fatigues. I am so going to get some.'

'Only when we rely on ourselves can we destroy the plutocratic corporatocracy that was once our country,' says the revolutionary leader. 'For centuries we have been herded like sheep to the voting booth, and for what? To choose a different colour put before us by the invisible government. All we are choosing is whether we want corporation written in blue, red, yellow or pink.'

There is cheering and applause. A person standing next to Terrence says to him, 'This is a bit radical for me. Sounds suspiciously like anarchism. Wouldn't we be better off going down the socialist democratic route like the Americans?'

'Perhaps,' says Terrence. 'But that option isn't available over here.'

'Does this leader have a name?'

'Known as Rosa to her/his friends.'

'Rosa?'

'Yes,' says Terrence. 'Named after Rosa Luxemburg. She was a Marxist theorist and revolutionary socialist at the turn of the 20th century. She/he is an ardent proponent of Luxemburgism.'

'Marxists were Bolsheviks, weren't they? We don't want a neo Stalin over here.'

'Luxemburgism is different,' says Terrence. 'It has a strong commitment to democracy.'

'Oh, look!'

Descending towards the crowd is a swimming pool sized thumbprint scanner carried by a brigade of drones. The scanner is dragged over the heads of the attendees, who cause a Mexican wave on leaping up into the air and declaring their support for the Revolution with a press of their thumbs.

Coup d'État

THE NEXT DAY – 10 DOWNING STREET – LONDON – The Prime Minister's wife is surprised when the doorbell rings, as no visitors are expected this morning. She approaches the door, opens it a fraction, sees the nose-ringed face of the Revolutionary Socialist leader, shrieks, and tries to close the door. The leader pushes the door forcefully. It opens. Behind her/him are thousands of her/his followers, engulfing the entire length and breadth of Downing Street.

A Mohawk-haired adviser, standing behind her/him on the doorstep, says, 'Get 'im doun 'ere nah!'

'But he's otherwise engaged; h-he's experiencing the cricket and isn't to be disturbed.'

'NAH!'

'Ally-Pally!' calls the Prime Minister's wife. '*Ally-Pally!*'

'What is it Wiffy? I'm frightfully busy experiencing the cricket.'

'There are some homeless people here to see you.'

'*Coming!*'

Moments later the Prime Minister approaches the front door. When he sees the Revolutionary Socialist leader, he says, 'Oh no, not you again! I'm frightfully busy experiencing the cricket and do not wish to be disturbed. Good day.' He tries to push the door closed but is prevented from doing so by her/his foot.

'It's over; I'm Prime Minister now,' says the Revolutionary Socialist leader.

'You are not a prime minister,' says the departing Prime Minister. 'You are a transgendered anarchist punk with a ring through your nose. Did you even go to Eton?'

The departing Prime Minister's wife is pulling at his sleeve. She says, 'Darling, Ally-Pally, I think we'd better go; there are thousands of them.'

Only now does the Prime Minister notice the horde of revolutionaries in the street. He gulps then says, 'Now, you listen here, you loathsome anarchist punk. I am the Prime Minister, not you.'

The revolutionaries boo.

'The people voted me in yesterday with their thumbs,' says the Revolutionary Socialist leader.

'Yes, I am aware of that, I do experience the news, you know,' says the departing Prime Minister. 'But your result is null and void.'

'How's that?'

'Only the government is permitted to use the population's biometric data. We gathered it, after all. And at any rate, you cannot hold impromptu elections. They happen every four years, and to be eligible to compete your party has to be selected by the plutocratic body representing the financial institutions and corporations. It is the same as cricket. If no part of the batsman's body or bat is grounded behind the popping—'

'You've got ten minutes,' says the Revolutionary Socialist leader.

'Right, Wiffy,' says the departing Prime Minister. 'Let's pack up and get out of here pronto before the revolutionaries decide to publicly execute us.'

'I'll get the silver cutlery, you pack up the pheasants in-flight engraved porcelain tea set.'

PLUTOCRAT TRIALS

MARCH 10TH, 2161 AD – NEW YORK SUPREME COURT – NEW YORK CITY – Inside, the latest plutocrat trial is underway. A couple of months back it was decreed that trials would no longer be televised in America, the Supreme Court having controversially ruled that the primary role of the judicial system is not to provide entertainment but to be seen to dispense justice. It is for this reason that reporters now congregate outside courts, even on days like today when a verdict is not due. Currently, there is a lone female Olde American-language broadcaster standing on the steps. Gesturing at the courthouse behind her, she says, 'Recent plutocrat trials have seen defendants argue that they were only following orders. Others have dismissed the label 'plutocrat' altogether, claiming they were merely capitalists. By appealing to the nation's traditional capitalist values, they hoped to endear themselves to the jury.

'Last month, during the Food Conglomerate Trials, the former chairman of the American Beef Industry argued that the belief in and the opportunity to generate and retain one's wealth was the principal reason for America having once been the greatest nation in the world. He was sentenced to liquidation. His co-conspirators were given life terms assisting the poor and clearing up environmental damage.

'So, what do we know about today's defendant? He is a 160-year-old former owner of Manhattan's most *amazing* bath—'

The door to the court springs open and a pink-faced man sporting a yellow mane races out, pursued by the court's security guards.

'Oh my *god!*' screeches the reporter.

'WOOO-ooo-OOO!' Walter rushes towards the steps. He

emits a 'WAHHHH!' as he does a two-footed jumping kung fu kick off the steps. But Walter, who has not had his anti-ageing medication in quite some time, lands awkwardly, falls over and topples down the remaining steps with a 'Wah wah ow wahhh!'

The security guards jump on top of Walter. The reporter, hurrying down the steps towards them, her drone camera in hot pursuit, reaches out with her microphone and says breathlessly, *'Disculpe. ¿Acaso usted … antiguo?'*

'No shit lady, I speak Olde American!' As Walter is carried by his arms and legs back to the courthouse he shouts, 'You hypocritical ass wipes! America's always been a plutocracy. Democracy was just a façade for making you believe you had a choice.'

The courthouse door slams shut.

THE FEDERAL RESERVE

THREE YEARS LATER – MAY 3RD, 2164 AD – CONSTITUTION AVENUE, WASHINGTON DC – The throng of visitors are touring the site of what was once the Eccles Building, the former headquarters of the Federal Reserve System. Destroyed during the Revolution, it is now a memorial to the Federal Reserve's millions of victims.

In the middle of the Memorial Garden, embedded in the ground, is the Federal Reserve System's plaque, a large circle with an eagle in the centre, its wings outstretched. There is a lengthy queue of people waiting in line for their chance to use this giant spittoon. A vacationing Canadian family, consisting of parents and their young son, are at the front of the queue.

'Hawk up that green stuff,' says the father to his son. 'Yeah, like that! Now go!'

The boy leans forward and expectorates on the plaque.

'Good boy!' says the mother.

A robotic janitor scurries onto the plaque, drags a mop across it and then beats a hasty retreat, narrowly avoiding a cascade of drool.

'Mom, Dad, why did everyone hate the Federal Reserve so much?' says the boy, looking imploringly up at his parents.

'Cos it was a member of the Axis of Evil,' says the father. 'Its policies enslaved countless millions of its own citizens.'

'And the Federal Reserve wasn't even part of the government, eh?' says the mother. 'And it was run by people who weren't elected, and it wasn't accountable to anyone.'

'And cos those brown-nosers were dominated by the Wall Street banks, they didn't give a damn about the people,' says the father. 'And they were the only ones allowed to create money. And they devalued the American dollar.'

The mother, crouching down in front of her son, says, 'We're real lucky we're Canadians not Americans.'

'Mom, Dad! Can I have ice cream?'

NEW LABOUR

THE SAME DAY – THE RED ROOM – 10 DOWNING STREET – LONDON
– The Prime Minister and several of her/his ministers and advisers
have been in a meeting all morning, here in what was once the
Terracotta Room, since renamed the Red Room, having been
repainted red. They are currently taking a mid-morning break.
The ministers and advisers, cups of tea in hand, talk idly amongst
each other. Meanwhile, the Prime Minister, perched on an
armchair by the room's ornamental fireplace, plays *Marxist
Renegade* on her/his mobile holophone.

A couple of metres away from where she/he sits, a female
minister is conversing with a government adviser. The adviser,
addressing the minister, says, 'Was it in the 1990s that the Labour
government abolished the death penalty?'

'No, it was in the 1960s, during the tenure of Harold Wilson.
His government also legalised homosexuality and abortion.'

'Oh,' says the adviser. 'I must have been getting myself
confused with that later Labour government, around the turn of
the millennium. You know, the ones with the social justice
agenda.'

The minister, having cast a glance in the direction of the Prime
Minister, draws her chair closer to the adviser and says in a quiet
voice, 'The Labour government you are referring to was in power
between 1997 and 2010. They were New Labour.'

'Yes, of course,' says the adviser. 'New Labour.'

'Socialist saboteurs!' shouts the Prime Minister.

'Prime Minister, are you r-referring to New Labour?' says the
startled adviser.

'Warmongers!' shouts the Prime Minister, now standing over
the adviser, looking down menacingly at him.

'Prime Minister, please,' implores the female minister.

The adviser, looking up at the Prime Minister wide-eyed, says, 'Prime Minister, I-I was just asking about New Labour.'

'Civil liberty annihilators! Leftist impersonators! Democracy deceivers!'

'Take it easy, Prime Minister,' says a minister on the other side of the room.

'Just *relax*,' says another.

The Prime Minister stands trembling, her/his fists clenched at her/his sides.

'I was j-j-just talking about the Labour party's h-history,' says the adviser.

Someone calls out, 'Don't say it!'

'I j-just m-mentioned,' says the adviser, 'New Labour.'

'PLUTOCRATIC PATRONS! PROPAGANDIST PARASITES! DUBYA'S DOORMAT!'

The adviser is poised to say something else when the female minister thrusts her hand over his mouth. Meanwhile, the rest of the room's occupants usher the Prime Minister back to her/his seat, the Prime Minister muttering, 'Warmongers, leftist impersonators, civil liberty annihilators,' as she/he goes.

Someone calls out, 'Find the Prime Minister's inhaler.'

Moments later a member of Downing Street's staff races through the room, inhaler in hand.

'Inhale,' says a minister, now crouched in front of the Prime Minister. 'Yes, there we go. *Relax*. It happened over a century and a half ago Prime Minister. We have to let it go.'

Workplace Democracy

OCTOBER 22ND, 2165 AD – PREFAB MANUFACTURER – GOTHENBURG – SWEDEN – The visiting man and woman are British trade union representatives. They are here in Sweden to learn about democracy in the workplace. At the present moment they are observing a line of workers assembling prefab boards. Noting that like the boards the workers appear identical to one another, and that they move at the same time as if synchronised, one of the trade union representatives says to her colleague, 'Are those workers robots?'

'No, they're Swedes.'

'Oh!'

Now pointing at a wheeled-machine, clasping prefabricated boards in its metallic arms, he says, 'That's a robot!'

'Yeah, I thought as much.' And then, leaning into her colleague, she whispers, 'These Swedes are so uniform. They've all got dark hair and—'

'Not that one!'

'Which one?'

'Two o'clock.'

Seeing the tall, blond-haired, blue-eyed male worker bent over a prefab board, electric drill in hand, she says, 'Are you sure he's a Swede?'

'I'm guessing he's an indigenous Swede … Stop staring!'

Their chaperon walks over and says, 'The democratically elected eco-manager will see you now.'

When the visitors enter the eco-manager's office, he greets them sombrely. The visitors sit down on chairs that they feel certain arrived flat-packed.

'So,' says the eco-manager, 'have you come here to learn English or to learn about democracy in the workplace?'

'Ha ha,' utters the male trade union representative.

'He he,' utters the female trade union representative.

Both were informed prior to arrival in the country that Swedes find the fact that they speak better English than the British very amusing.

'You did not respond to my question, so I will progress on the assumption that you are here to learn about democracy in the workplace. Us Swedes are unable to fathom how it has taken so long for primitive nations like yourselves to understand that democracy isn't only for election day. For democracy to work it must encompass every facet of life. Do you know when democracy in the workplace was first introduced here in Sweden?'

The trade union representatives shake their heads.

'Two hundred years ago. Two decades before our ancestors started arriving here in meaningful numbers, first from the Balkans, later from the Horn of Africa and Syria. At that time the hospitable native population passed labour laws that led to industrial democracy. This meant that workers voted on deciding what happened in the workplace. Unfortunately, it was evident in the economic downturn in the late 1970s and early '80s that some of these well-meaning measures had been excessive.

'After that, we entered the dark ages, reverting to primitive, greedy, consumerist corporate types like yourselves. Well, not that bad, but you get my point.'

'Tosser!' mutters the male trade union representative.

'Excuse me?'

'Nothing.'

'In recent years we have been steadily bringing back democracy to the workplace but, and this is crucial,' says the eco-manager, raising his right index finger, 'using technological advances to cut out the bureaucracy whilst at the same time keeping human workers for many tasks, allowing workplace democracy to flourish but making sure it does not adversely affect production or performance. In fact, you could say that by bringing back this ancient practice, we are, as you say in English … being atavistic.'

The trade union representatives do not know what atavistic means, but they don't let on.

Burger Flipper

FEBRUARY 21ST, 2166 AD – MCDONALD'S – HOLBORN, LONDON –
119-year-old Terrence is eating lunch. Having taken a slurp of his
responsibly sweetened soft drink, he has a bite of his synthetic,
environment-loving double cheese, we're so sorry about yesterday
we're now a caring corporation faux beef burger. *This might be one
sanctimonious burger*, thinks Terrence to himself, *but it tastes
really good.*

On an adjoining table a pair of burger-munching lawyers are
observing a robot, with spatulas for hands, flipping burgers on a
grill. After taking a slurp of their soft drink, one of the lawyers
says, 'Humans used to do that job, flipping burgers.'

'Yes,' says the other lawyer, 'it must have been the most tedious
job ever.'

'The law would give it a run for its money.'

'That's as maybe, but at least senior corporate, ethically paid
lawyers like ourselves will not be replaced by automation
technology robots slash artificial intelligence.'

'You will be,' calls out Terrence. 'The law is, after all, process-
driven, repetitive, largely administrative, predictable and does not
require empathy. Human lawyers are destined for the scrapheap.'

DEATH DAY

When the elderly woman enters the café a customer says to her, 'Your death day must be coming up very soon.'

'Yes, I will be 160 tomorrow. Thank you for remembering.'

Another customer walks over and says, 'Was hoping I'd find you in here. I got you this Happy Death Day card for tomorrow.'

'Oh, thank you, how thoughtful.'

'My pleasure! So, what's the plan for the big day?'

'Travelling out to Zurich with the family first thing in the morning. Got a birthday slash death day lunch at a restaurant with lovely views of the lake. Living funeral starts at four. Looking to depart about four-thirty quarter to five, all being well.'

'Lethal injection, is it?'

'I suspect so. Haven't checked the details yet.'

The soon-to-be 160-year-old is inspecting the assortment of cakes behind the counter when the café's owner emerges from the kitchen and says, 'Afternoon. It's your death day tomorrow, isn't it? How are you feeling?'

'Feeling fine, thank you for asking. And yes, tomorrow is the big day.'

'No regrets?'

'None whatsoever. I've done an awful lot in my time, both real and virtual. It's time to move on.'

'But you're in such fine fettle, other than being a bit wizened.'

'Yes, it's a bit of a shame bowing out when I'm still as fit as a fiddle. But they're the rules, aren't they? When you turn 160 in this country it's time for the chop. There's no point hanging around anyway. All I'd be doing is taking up resources meant for the young'uns.'

'I'd be feeling pretty nervous if it were me,' says the café owner.

'Me too!' says a customer.

'Petrified,' says another customer. 'Absolutely petrified.'

The café owner says, 'Which interment option are you going with?'

'Carrot cake, to go.'

GRIM REAPER

THE FOLLOWING WEEK – THE CROWN COURT – LONDON – The legal age limit is 160. The defendant is 161. A team of human barristers, hired by the defendant, have been fighting to have their client exempted from this law. Their defence rests on the premise that their client's altruistic life means she is of more worth to her fellow citizens alive than dead. For much of the morning the defendant's barristers have been presenting their case. The judge, like her predecessors of yesteryear who presided over civil cases, wears a black gown. This traditional outfit has now been augmented with a black hood.

When the defence has finished its presentation, the defendant rises to her feet and addresses the judge.

'It is imperative for the welfare of the nation that I be granted permission to indefinitely extend my productive, righteous and altruistic life.'

'Take a tea break in the anteroom,' says the judge. 'You will be summoned when I have reached my verdict. This—'

'I do not tolerate caffeine. I require rooibos tea.'

The judge brings her gavel down against the wooden block repeatedly, the sound reverberating through the court. She says, 'Tea requests are to be addressed to the mechanised maids, not me.'

The defendant is poised to make another tea-related comment when her barristers usher her out of the courtroom. An evidence collation drone comes sibilating through the courtroom. When the judge says, 'Evidence!', a thin band of horizontal red light shoots out of the drone and scans the judge's pupils. The drone soars upwards towards the ceiling and beams down a holographic board on the table in front of the judge, in a manner similar to the projectors of earlier centuries. With its coloured rectangles, miniature houses and cars, the hologram resembles a Monopoly board.

'Now, let us find out whether the defendant is worthy of the contemporary equivalent of canonisation that is extended life.'

The judge, having rearranged her hood, leans forward and inspects the evidence. The judge taps the roof of the largest of the Monopoly-type houses. This is the defendant's primary residence. The house expands, taking up the whole of the table. The judge's attention is drawn to a blue rectangular shape in the house's grounds. This is the property's private swimming pool.

The judge is inspecting the board again. There is a £ icon on the board. When she presses it a pie chart outlining the defendant's average annual expenditure materialises.

'Bloody hell!'

The judge continues to scrutinise the evidence.

Twenty minutes later – When the defendant is escorted back to her seat in the courtroom the judge says, 'Did you find rooibos tea?'

'No, I did not. It is incredibly important—'

The defendant is silenced by one of her barristers placing his hand over her mouth. He says, 'Have you reached a verdict, Your Honour?'

'Yes.'

'Our client, what is to be her fate?'

'Incineration!'

RA'S ABOMINATION

DECEMBER 1ST, 2170 AD – AN INCARCERATION POD – SOUTHPORT CORRECTIONAL FACILITY – NEW YORK STATE – AMERICA – The fading sun casts a reddish hue, silhouetting the pyramids, palm trees and the birds teeming in the sky. Below in the great river a surfacing Nile perch sends ripples coursing across the water. Descending through the air is a flock of marbled teal. Having landed with a plop they emit faint *eeeps* as they swim towards a cluster of papyrus on the near bank. High above, the symbol for eternal life, the ankh, is illuminating as a star constellation.

The bathroom door slides open and the two wives enter on all fours in feline-fashion, their white, Ancient Egyptian-style dresses clinging to their lithe bodies. Having stationed themselves on their knees on either side of the bath, one of the wives reaches forward and strokes Walter's cheek with her fingertips.

'Woooo.'

Walter feels the stroking sensation even as his eyelids flutter, and he awakens in his single-person incarceration pod. The lid has come off and a rat is leaning in, its whiskers tingling his cheek.

'Wahhh!' shrieks Walter, recoiling from Ra's abomination[3].

---

[3] Rats were so reviled in the Ancient Egyptian world that they were referred to as the creator Ra's abomination.

III: ESCHATOLOGY

Accountants Quandary

APRIL 6TH, 2171 AD – A DRINKS PARTY – BASINGSTOKE – 124-year-old Terrence takes a sip of Finnish Pinot Noir before nibbling on a synthetic cheese cube and cucumber on a stick hors d'oeuvre. Four years ago, Terrence finally reached the ever-increasing mandatory retirement age of 120. He is now a gentleman of leisure. A conversation is underway close to where Terrence is standing. He is listening in.

A female guest, addressing a fellow guest, says, 'So, I hear you're currently on your midlife sabbatical. How fun … What is it that you do for work?'

The man hurriedly swallows a partially chewed synthetic cheese cube before saying, 'I am a CPA, a certified public accountant.'

'And how long have you been doing that?'

'Sixty years.'

'Six decades of accountancy! It hurts just saying it.'

Terrence chuckles. The two guests are looking at Terrence.

'Did I say something funny?' says the female guest.

'No,' says Terrence. 'A synthetic cheese cube going down the wrong way caused me to choke. Well, it might have been a piece of cucumber.'

The female guest resumes her conversation with her fellow guest. She says, 'Surely you are not planning on going back to your CPA job after your sabbatical? You must be sick to death of accountancy after six decades.'

'Well, assuming that I am not replaced by artificial intelligence, I have another three decades to go.'

The female guest groans. She says, 'What exactly does being a CPA entail?'

'It entails skills such as sequential organising, making logical, objective decisions and being detail orientated. The activities are really quite varied. Working on internal control systems, compliance audits, investigative audits and financial audits. The eight steps in the monthly accounting cycle must be considered at all times. Namely transactions, journal entries, posting, trial balance—'

'Euthanasia!'

'Excuse me?'

'Euthanasia,' repeats the female guest. 'As a midlife sabbatical-taker you are eligible for euthanasia[4]. A painless injection and it's all over.'

'Well, I-I don't know.'

'Oh, you must!'

'Where are the synthetic cheese cube and cucumber on a stick hors d'oeuvres?' says the male guest. 'Ah, there they are.'

He walks off. Terrence, reflecting on his near century-long career, considers that he might have opted for the mid-working life euthanasia option, had it been available at the time. But he concludes that he is happy to still be alive, unlike his plutocrat American relative Walter who died in December of last year of a heart attack in prison. A smile forms on Terrence's face. A woman holding a plate approaches Terrence. She says, 'Is something amusing you?'

'No.'

'Can I interest you in an hors d'oeuvre?'

Peering down at the cake-shaped hors d'oeuvres, Terrence says, 'What are they?'

'Mini crab substitute cakes with eco pineapple–cucumber salsa. Would you like one?'

'Why not, you only live once.'

---

[4] Burdened by state pension contributions, the government offers a get-out-of-work clause. This entails working for six decades or so before taking a break. Then, instead of returning to the workplace, opting for state-sponsored, no judgment attached, tax incentive laden euthanasia.

WINTER FROLICS

FEBRUARY 19TH, 2172 AD – THE ALPS – FRANCE – The rotorcraft's passengers are peering out of the windows at Chamonix's grass-covered slopes. The golden age of ski tourism is but a distant memory.

The passengers, their faces pressed to the windows, scour the jagged peaks of the mountains that surround the Chamonix Valley. Someone shrieks, '*SNOW!*'

Eager eyes follow the direction of the shrieker's prodding finger. The interior of the rotorcraft erupts in vociferations of glee when the passengers catch sight of the white-tipped peak of Mont Blanc, the highest peak in Western Europe and the last remaining refuge for snow.

As the rotorcraft descends, its passengers hastily attach skis and snowboards to their feet. A passenger says to the pilot, 'Hurry up!'

'Let's do this!' shouts a passenger, pounding the side of the rotorcraft with their fists.

The back of the rotorcraft is opening.

'One at a time,' says the pilot.

The request is ignored by the bevy of off-piste thrill-seekers stampeding towards the back of the rotorcraft. Having leapt to the ground they shoot off down the mountain slope, discharging celebratory whooping noises as they go. Within a matter of seconds they have slid to a halt in a pool of grey slush, where under a resplendent blue sky they hug each other and dance around in circles.

FAITH

JUNE 24TH, 2173 AD – A CLASSROOM – SOMEWHERE – 'After Jesus died on the cross he was buried in a tomb. Three days later he rose again,' says the cultural studies teacher. 'This was a miracle.'

'*Hello*, that's not a miracle, that's cryogenics,' says a girl.

A boy near the back of the class, says, 'Stupid ho, there was no cryogenics back then.'

'*Excuse me,*' says the girl. 'Cryogenics has been around like forever.'

'There was no cryogenics in Jesus's time,' says the teacher.

'Oh, there wasn't? *Sorry.*'

'Maybe Jesus made a secret cold-storage cryogenics facility that no one knew about,' says another student.

'Or it was just really cold like a cryogenics place. And then someone took Jesus out of there and he was alive again.'

The teacher shakes his head. He says nothing. A girl raises her hand.

'Yes, Lambrini?'

'People have been resurrected after like half a century and we don't worship them. Jesus only did three days.'

The teacher, looking up at the ceiling, ponders his response. He says, 'Jesus's resurrection was a miracle because it surpassed all known human and natural powers of the time.'

'*Bullshit!*'

'Language,' says the teacher. 'And besides, in addition to the Resurrection, Jesus also performed many other miracles.'

A student says, 'These primitive people thought the World was flat. They didn't even have electricity. Their observations and interpretations don't count for much.'

'Faith,' says the teacher. 'Do you know what faith is?'

'Sure, I know what superstition is.'

The teacher is poised to respond, when a girl says, 'Just because people said Jesus did some stuff don't make it true.'

'Yeah,' concur several of her classmates.

'We hear, see, smell and touch in our virtual-reality worlds every day,' says the girl. 'Does that mean they are real?'

'No,' says the teacher. 'They're an illusion.'

'Illusion is one step ahead of delusion.'

DODOS

APRIL 22ND, 2174 AD – MAURITIUS – The presenter is standing on a podium in the middle of the forest clearing. Having surveyed the audience gathered in a circle around her, she says, 'In 2003 a cloned female Pyrenean ibex became the first species ever to be brought back from extinction. Unfortunately, it lived for only a couple of minutes before succumbing to a lung defect.'

'Ahhh.'

'Recent years have seen scientific breakthroughs result in genetic samples harvested from extinct species' specimens being used to bring a number of species back from the dead.'

Some members of the audience fiddle with the stems of their champagne flutes, others shift their weight from one foot to the other.

'*Raphus cucullatus* was a large flightless bird once endemic on Mauritius,' continues the presenter. 'Discovered in the 1590s, it was pronounced extinct in 1681. Today, we, in partnership with the Mauritius Tourist Board, are proud to present to you *Raphus cucullatus*, more commonly known as the dodo.'

There is a large object draped in a cloth at the edge of the forest clearing. The cloth is whipped off, revealing a cage. The cage door opens. Then nothing.

'Come on,' says someone in the audience, 'we haven't got all day.'

A black tip appears at the cage door, followed by a long yellow beak. When the naked head emerges, there is rapturous applause and cheering. With a loud squawk the metre-tall, grey-plumaged symbol of obsolescence steps out of the cage and into its natural habitat, for the first time in nearly 500 years.

'I just knew they had grey plumage,' says a champagne flute-clasping onlooker.

'Look,' says another. 'It isn't afraid of humans, even after everything that happened.'

A second dodo, emerging from the cage, tilts its head and inquisitively inspects the circled onlookers. Specimens continue to file out until there are five dodos standing in a line.

An attendee says, 'This is the best thing to happen to ecotourism since the invention of the eco hut.'

The lead dodo rotates its cumbersome frame around 180-degrees and proceeds to walk back towards the cage, followed by its companions. The audience laughs. Someone says, 'Don't go back to the cage, you silly birds; you're free now.'

POLITICAL SYSTEM

SEPTEMBER 1ST, 2175 AD – BASINGSTOKE – Terrence is talking to a former work associate on the holophone. He says, 'The entire political system is about to be overhauled, mark my words.'

'What are you talking about? It's only just been overhauled.'

'Yes, and for the better by and large. But another overhaul is imminent. Politicians are going to be replaced by artificial intelligence.'

'No way! We wouldn't have had a revolution if all we're going to do is cede control to artificial intelligence, would we?'

'Yes, we would.'

'Why?'

'Because,' says Terrence, 'now we can program artificial intelligence to govern us with a top down moral motivational system that is designed for the universal good and is free from materialism and greed. Prior to the overthrow of the plutocracies, oligarchies and corporatocracies, this would have been impossible.'

'Oh, I see what you're saying. Whoever programs the artificial intelligence system that's going to rule us, knows the code can be trusted and that there are no Trojan horses hidden in it.'

'Exactly!'

'But are we really ready to be governed by artificial intelligence?'

'It is inevitable anyway. Better to programme the system whilst we are still in a position to. At any rate, artificial intelligence is focused, rational and error free, unlike politicians.'

'I'm not sure. Putting aside politicians' deceit and rampant lying, they are at least human. And that makes them the same as us, unlike artificial intelligence.'

'Listen to this analogy,' says Terrence. 'If one of our ancestors way back was waiting to board an aeroplane and they were informed that their flight was to be pilotless, what would their reaction have been?'

'Panic, most likely. They might well not have boarded the plane.'

'Exactly. But what if you boarded an aeroplane today and discovered a human pilot behind the wheel. What would your reaction be?'

'Panic, obviously. Humans make errors. There used to be plane crashes back when there were human pilots.'

VIRTUAL-REALITY TELEVISION

AUGUST 16TH, 2176 AD - A RESIDENTIAL HOME - MAIDSTONE, KENT - ENGLAND - The retiree is currently having an afternoon snooze, something he doesn't generally do, but he wants to be well rested for the primetime, virtual-reality, celebrity reality television programme at five. Until the recent introduction of this particular programme, he had abhorred celebrity reality television his entire life. He had first been subjected to it as a small child in the family home. Over the years he had witnessed a plethora of virtual-reality, celebrity reality television shows that had catered to the vicarious, the voyeur, the vain and the vapid. There had been *Celebrity Big Brother*-style shows, set in a host of locations, including historical re-enactments in landmarks such as the Tower of London and the Palace of Versailles; these, in addition to dancing with B-list celebrities and a raft of survivor-style programmes in jungles, deserts, mountainous regions, underwater and even on the moon. As well as the aforementioned, or in combination with, had been boot camp incarcerated obese celebrities, bulimic celebrities, comeback celebrities, cooking celebrities, recovering drug-addicted celebrities, transgendered celebrities, vertically challenged celebrities and ideologically conflicting celebrities. Virtual-reality, celebrity reality television shows had been the cause of one of this retiree's divorces, and a significant factor in another.

From the direction of the recreation room, an ebullient, female, high-pitched Liverpudlian-accented voice shrieks, 'Five minutes to go, like!'

The retiree leaps out of bed, inserts his feet into his slippers, grabs his dressing gown from the hook on the back of the door and departs in haste.

Now in the recreation room, the retiree scans the rows of reclining armchairs. Having located a place near the front he makes his way through the bustling, cacophonous mass of residents. When he sits down an elderly woman in the adjacent seat, says, 'Hello, how's it going?'

'Not bad. When's your heart transplant?'

'Tuesday.'

A pair of mechanised maids, trawling the rows of reclining armchairs, hand out mugs of tea and custard cream biscuits. The retirees reach up and pull their chairs' built-in virtual-reality helmets down, but only to their brows, so as to be able to maintain eye contact until the commencement of the programme. The helmets worn in this manner resemble the hairdryers found in 1950s' hair salons.

The retirement home's human manager enters the room and says breathlessly, 'Phew, I made it just in time. Pull your helmets down, everyone; we're ready to go.'

The retirees pull down their virtual-reality helmets. A moment later they are thrust into an empty stadium, where a buxom Latin pop queen, clad in a vest and fluorescent-pink Muay Thai shorts, is racing up the stadium's steps under a blazing sun. At the bottom of the steps her trainer, having glanced at his stopwatch, bellows in an American accent, '¡RÁPIDO! ¡RÁPIDO!'

The scene disintegrates. Another appears. Beneath a grey sky is a field, where a tattooed British female grunge revival singer is pulling an antiquated car tyre through the mud, watched uninterestedly by a cow, and her trainer, who barks out, 'Come on, no pain no gain!'

These two singers' rivalry had begun the previous year when the grunge revival singer had taken issue with the pink Spandex outfit the Latin pop queen had worn to the MTV Awards. She had compared it to a trifle on social media, the message complete with the #pudding. A ferocious social media war had ensued between the stars and their hordes of adoring fans. This Saturday the feud will be settled in the MGM Grand in Las Vegas, Nevada, in the eight-sided cage that is the Octagon.

The retiree takes to wondering what would have happened if the bickering stars of yesteryear had settled their differences in the cage. A smile flickers across his face when he imagines what a great matchup silver-screen stars and sworn enemies Bette Davis and Joan Crawford would have made, or Madonna and Elton John, or Nicki Minaj and Mariah Carey.

ARTIFICIAL INTELLIGENCE

MAY 30TH, 2177 AD – ARTIFICIAL INTELLIGENCE (AI) CONFERENCE – VANCOUVER – CANADA – 'HG Wells and Aldous Huxley were warning us about the threat posed by machines way back in the early 20th century. Now it is a reality,' says the conference's organiser. 'Computers being limited to specific tasks is but a distant memory. Today they manage our financial markets, transport systems, our entire economies. These individual supercomputers are communicating with each other. It is inevitable that tomorrow they will form a single AI ecosystem, controlling every facet of human existence.

'The issue we must address is what course of action we are to take in the unfortunate event that this soon-to-be near-omnipotent supercomputer fails to act in our own interests?' An audience member puts their hand up. 'Yes, what is your suggestion?'

'Unplug the computer.'

CREEPY CRAWLIES

MARCH 21ST, 2178 AD – A RESTAURANT – HAMPSHIRE – ENGLAND –
Terrence is sitting alone at a table, inspecting the menu. A wheeled
robotic waiter is scooting in his direction. When a woman shouts,
'Waiter, waiter!', it changes course and scoots over to her table. The
robotic waiter says, 'Are you ready to order?'

'Um … I will go with the … the … Are your maggots
responsibly harvested?'

'Yes,' says the robotic waiter. 'We use bluebottle larvae raised
on organic animal manure.'

'Perfect. In that case I will go with the synthetic Stilton-stuffed
maggots …'

Having pulled up beside Terrence's table the waiter says, 'Are
you ready to order?'

'What would you recommend?'

'The savoury, sustainable farming, organic buckwheat crêpes
with maggot fat.'

Terrence scrunches up his face. He says, 'No, I don't think so. I
will go with the … faux Beef Wellington with environmentally
friendly new potatoes and recycled-water-sourced lettuce leaves.'

Golden Years

JUNE 25TH, 2179 AD – VITALITY RETIREMENT HOME – POLEGATE, EAST SUSSEX – ENGLAND – The elderly people sitting in the rows of chairs converse with one another, sip tea and nibble biscuits. The door bursts open. An all-in-one, faux silk suit clad salesman strides into the room and greets his audience with an enthusiastic, 'Morning, ladies, gentlemen and trans people.'

Some of the attendees mumble in reciprocation. The grinning salesman is now standing on a podium at the front of the room. When he clicks his fingers, a metre-high hologrammed single-column bar chart materialises beside him. Gesturing at the chart with one hand, he says, 'In 2020, approximately 19.3% of the UK's population were of retirement age.' He clicks his fingers again. A second bar appears, soaring upwards towards the ceiling, dwarfing its neighbour by many metres. 'Today, 33% of the population are retirees.'

Yawns are audible and groans too. A woman screeches, 'We know all about it love.'

'Yeah,' says another. 'We've been informed; we experience the news every day, several times a day in fact.'

A man shouts, 'And some of us experience *The Economist!*'

'So, you are all aware that the increase is even more dramatic when one considers that in 2020 the retirement age was 66. Today it is 120.'

'Yeah, we know that.'

'Get to the point; we haven't got all day!'

'I am a representative of Nirvana UK,' continues the salesman. 'We, Nirvana UK, have one obsession. To provide the highest level of living standards for our nation's elderly. We have recently forged a partnership with the government to provide a solution to the ageing crisis. Is everything clear so far?'

There are muttered *yeses* and yawns too.

'I am here today to offer you a revolutionary way to see out your days. We, Nirvana UK, have combined the latest advances in virtual reality and neuroscience to give you, the ageing population of this once great nation, the—'

'Just get to the point!'

The salesman swallows. He says, 'Basically, this place, Vitality Retirement Home, has been err ... earmarked for sea defences, and you're all going to be moved elsewhere.'

'This is an outrage!' shouts a man with quivering jowls.

'Preposterous!' shouts another, his countenance turning instantaneously crimson.

'Scandalous!' exclaims a biodegradable walking stick shaking woman.

The sound of dissenting voices and chair legs scraping against the floor fills the room. The salesman, holding out his palms in front of him, says, 'Please, just hear me out on this.'

Those attendees shuffling towards the exit exude huffing noises and return to their seats. Someone says, 'To where do you propose we are to be moved?'

'Yes, please tell?'

'As you know,' says the salesman, 'there is virtually no free space on this crammed island of ours. And what little there is has been earmarked for other things.'

'What're you offering us?' says the woman with the biodegradable walking stick, which is now pointing menacingly in the salesman's direction.

'You are going to love what we have in store for you. We are going to make your dreams come true—'

'Don't tell us, show us,' says an elderly woman in the middle rows.

'Very well,' says the salesman. After inhaling deeply, he clicks his fingers. A small hologram, about the size of an A4 pad, materialises beside him, where the bar chart had been.

'BIGGER!' shouts *The Economist* experiencer.

The salesman draws his outstretched hands a little further apart. The hologram expands slightly.

'How can we see that?'

'It's too small.'

'BIGGER!'

When the salesman draws his outstretched hands further apart, the hologram expands. The audience stares wide-eyed at the hologram of a transparent box, longer than it is wide. Meanwhile, the salesman braces himself for the anticipated outpouring of protestation.

A man shouting, 'I'm not spending the rest of my days in a box!', is followed by a cacophony of dissenting voices, boos, and thrown objects too. The salesman ducks, narrowly avoiding a half-eaten digestive biscuit, then deftly moves his head to the side as a teacup flies past and shatters against the wall. Someone shouts, 'It's a coffin!'

The Economist experiencer says, 'I didn't spend the best part of a century in the workplace so I could end up in a coffin.'

The salesman says, 'The fact that Paradise Pods have the same dimensions as a standard UK coffin is incidental.'

Meaning of Life

AUGUST 7TH, 2180 AD – AN ALPHA COURSE MEETING –
SOMEWHERE – The title of this evening's session is *Reconciling Artificial Intelligence and Christianity*. The talk is now over and question time is underway. An attendee says, 'Most of us are aware that we are in the process of being overtaken as the dominant species on this planet by artificially intelligent supercomputers. My question is, do you think that this artificial intelligence is God?'

'God works in mysterious ways,' says the course organiser.

An attendee says, 'That is a vague and wholly inadequate response.'

The course organiser is poised to elaborate when someone says, 'If this supercomputer has a higher intelligence than us, it must be God.'

'I agree,' says another attendee. 'The only explanation is that this supercomputer thingy must be God, Jesus and the Holy Spirit rolled into one.'

'What we don't understand, we can make mean anything.'

PARADISE PODS

JANUARY 10TH, 2181 AD – A RETIREMENT HOME – EASTBOURNE, EAST SUSSEX – 'The fact that Paradise Pods have the same dimensions as a standard coffin is incidental,' says the salesman, ducking to avoid the hurled teacup.

'It's a coffin!' shouts one of the elderly attendees.

A biodegradable walking stick wielding woman shouts, 'Shut it! Let 'im get on with it. There's only fourteen mins until *Celebrity Matchmaker!*'

The room falls silent. The salesman, gesturing at the hologram of a transparent box beside him, says, 'Paradise Pods are cushioned and heated as standard. With regards sustenance, you'll be fed on a nutritious diet of spirulina sea algae through here.' When he clicks his fingers a hologram of a luminous-green pipe penetrates the top of the box. 'Waste material will be removed through here.'

Another pipe appears, this one emerging from the base of the box.

'I don't want to see out my days in a Paradise Pod!' shrieks a woman in the middle rows.

'Yes you do,' says the salesman. 'Now, raise your hands if you like virtual-reality experiences?' Hands shoot up in the air. 'So, what's the problem? You'll be seeing out your days in the virtual-reality realm.

'We've got loads of experiences to choose from. Take the four tranquil pre-global warming scenarios, for instance. And for all of you who aren't ready to leave life in the fast lane quite yet, there are numerous top-end city locations, including Ancient Rome, late 20th-century Manhattan and early 21st-century Sydney harbour side.' He surveys the elderly attendees. 'Who likes fresh mountain air, lakes and log cabins?'

Several hands are raised. Someone says, 'They're alright.'

The elderly residents proceed to chatter to one another.

The biodegradable walking stick wielding woman stands up and says, 'Let 'im finish. There's only eleven mins until *Celebrity Matchmaker!*'

'Thank you,' says the salesman. 'Now, let me take some questions … Yes, you sir, at the front.'

'What about our friends and families? When will we see 'em?'

'It will work like this. You will be kept in a comatose state in your Paradise Pods, living the dream. Every Saturday afternoon at three you will be awakened from your slumber …

FUSSY EATERS

FEBRUARY 3RD, 2182 AD – 18B CLAYTON CRESCENT, BASINGSTOKE – Having recently undergone a heart transplant, 135-year-old Terrence is acutely aware of his own mortality. Although he is now feeling as right as rain, he knows that he has a finite number of good years left. Terrence is determined to live a little whilst he still can, hence his decision to go to Belgium on a weekend foray.

Terrence is in the process of booking his flight. He is currently inspecting the airline's in-flight meal dietary requirements form.

Please select your in-flight meal requirements from the list below:

Algae Meal - Alkaline Diet Meal - Baby Meal - Blood Type A Specific Meal - Blood Type B Specific Meal - Blood Type AB Specific Meal - Blood Type O Specific Meal. *This is all rather specific.* Celebrity Crash Diet Meal - Child Meal - Environmental Apologist Meal. *No, I have had quite enough environmental apologist meals for one lifetime.*

Fermented Food Meal - Fruitarian Meal - Gluten Intolerant Meal - Low Calorie Meal … Meat (entomophagist – insect) Meal. *Yuck.* Meat Meal (red meat) – N/A (for environmental reasons Air Channel Hopper does not serve or permit the consumption of red meat on-board its flights). *So why mention it, you sanctimonious …?* Meat Meal (organic, humane, responsibly sourced poultry). *Sounds promising; count me in.*

Meat Meal (pescatarian – fish) - Meat Meal (synthetic) - Pill Only Meal - Vegan Meal … Sonic-Enhanced Meals (please note that all the above options are available as sonic-enhanced meals. The applicable music/sounds will be provided through your personal in-flight entertainment system)

Terrence considers that lists never used to be this confounding when he was young. Then he remembers a sexual orientation question he had once been confronted with whilst filling out a job application over a century earlier in 2077.

ASTEROID

APRIL 29TH, 2183 AD - SPACE - The astronaut, peering through the window of the spacecraft, sees a lump of rock hurtling through space. Addressing his colleague, he says, 'Can you see that asteroid?'

'Yeah, I can,' she says. 'Its name is Bennu.'

'Bennu?'

'Come on, you're an astronaut, you must have heard of Bennu. Bennu is a carbonaceous asteroid with a diameter of 492 metres (1,614 ft; 0.306 mi). It was discovered by the LINEAR Project on September 11th, 1999.'

'Oh yeah, I remember now! Bennu's one of those asteroids that was predicted to possibly hit Earth. That wouldn't have been good. It could have changed life there forever.'

'Bennu had the second-highest rating on the Palermo Technical Impact Hazard Scale, with a one in 2,700 chance of impacting Earth.'

'You really paid attention in training, huh? When was Bennu predicted to collide with Earth?'

'The end of the 22nd century.'

'Round about now then.'

'Yes. But we are not in the clear. There are other asteroids out there. Bigger ones!'

UNITED NATIONS

JULY 24TH, 2184 AD – UNITED NATIONS HEADQUARTERS – NEW YORK CITY – The Secretary General, addressing the General Assembly, says, 'It has been apparent for many years that the human race would eventually be superseded by a supercomputer. That day is nearly upon us. We will soon be governed by the supercomputer's algorithms.'

'NO!' says a delegate. 'We must not allow ourselves to be governed by algorithms!'

'We already are,' says another delegate. 'Have been since the early 2000s when our species was dominated by Google Search, Facebook's News Feed and the National Security Agency (NSA).'

Occupations

MAY 18TH, 2185 AD – A TRAIN – SOMEWHERE – The young girl is studying a list of job titles on her holographic device for a history test. Rotating her pig-tailed head towards her father in the adjacent seat, she says, 'What were surgeons?'

'Surgeons were doctors who performed surgical procedures.'

'What were dentists?'

'Dentists were tooth doctors.'

'What were lawyers?'

'Professionals employed in the legal profession. I think you could have worked that one out for yourself.'

'Accountants?'

'Dreary sorts who inspected and audited accounts.'

'Were you an accountant?'

'No.'

'What were hairdressers?'

'People who cut hair. There are still a fair few hairdressers around today. It's a peculiar phenomenon. Some people don't like having their hair cut by robots. It's quite a personal act, I suppose.'

'Fishermen?'

'People who caught fish.'

'Delivery men/women/trans people?'

'People who delivered things.'

'Vets?'

'Animal doctors.'

'Dad?'

'Yes.'

'Are we nearly there yet?'

School of Thought

MARCH 3RD, 2186 AD – SOMEWHERE – The two people have been arguing for quite some time.

'The Commodore 64 was the biggest-selling computer model ever, *okay*. Unlike its competitors it—'

'Like I don't already know that! What you're conveniently forgetting is that the Atari 2600—'

'Excuse me! I didn't interrupt you, so at least have the decency to do the same.'

'Whatever!'

'The Commodore 64's eight-bit home computer changed human history. Unlike its—'

'What you're omitting to mention is that—'

'Stop interrupting! What is the point in trying to explain these historical facts if you're so ignorant about everything?'

'Ignorant, excuse me. You're the one—'

'UNLIKE ITS COMPETITORS the Commodore 64 made its documentation available to its disciples. Why did the Commodore 64 do this? Because its documentation was the truth, that's why. The others were not, *okay*? That's how the good news spread everywhere.'

'Hello! What you're forgetting is that the Atari 2600 came first. And—'

'I know that; if you'd been listening I—'

'Stop interrupting! You are so annoying and wrong.'

'Me? No, *you!*'

'The Atari 2600 was a miracle maker. Firstly, it was the first home console. And it had Pac-Man, which was really important culturally. Not only that but it had a 15-year lifespan. And—'

'Lifespan has—'

'Excuse me, I haven't finished yet! The Atari 2600 popularised the use of microprocessor-based hardware and ROM cartridges.'

'If you'd checked your facts you would know what happened. What the Atari 2600 was actually doing – and this is a fact *okay*? The Atari 2600 was a prophet anticipating the coming of the Commodore 64.'

GHOST TOWNS

AUGUST 3RD, 2187 AD – INTERSTATE 94 – RURAL NORTH DAKOTA – AMERICA – Two tourists, a father and daughter, are travelling in a self-drive rental car along Interstate 94. The daughter, looking out through the car's window, sees an abandoned gas station, several derelict buildings with towering weeds growing out front and a vacant diner with smashed windows. The girl says, 'Daddy, look, another deserted town. Why are there so many towns like this around here?'

'It is because of self-drive trucks darling.'

'What have self-drive trucks got to do with it?'

'Before self-drive trucks, truck driving was the job done by more people than any other in many states. Back in the early 21st century there were 3.5 million truck drivers in America. Whole towns like this one depended on those truck drivers. I'm talking gas stations, diners, motels ...'

ARMAMENTS

JUNE 30TH, 2188 AD – A NUCLEAR WEAPONS INSTALLATION – SOMEWHERE – The soldier presses a button on the controller's keyboard. Nothing happens. She presses it again. Nothing. She presses a different button, then another. Nothing.

'General!' shouts the soldier as she races from the room. Moments later she rushes back into the room, the general at her heels. 'The PS7 nuclear bomb machine-gun controller isn't responding,' says the soldier, pressing a button on the keyboard. 'Look, nothing's happening; the green light isn't appearing on the holographic screen.'

The general barges the soldier out of the way. He prods the button, then another button.

'NOO!' he shouts. 'The Supercomputer must have taken over the defence grid.'

ECOTOURISM

JULY 13TH, 2189 AD – MONTEVERDE, CENTRAL HIGHLANDS – COSTA RICA – Trampling through the cloud forest is an ecotourist and her human guide. They are heading to the most secluded part of the forest in the hope of seeing quetzal birds, three-wattled bellbirds and hummingbirds, of which there are many different types, though less than back in the day.

Hearing a chirping somewhere high up in the canopy, the ecotourist exclaims, 'That is the call of the quetzal! I would recognise it anywhere.'

She heads off in the direction of the call, stamping through the dense foliage, her drone camera buzzing at her shoulder like a giant bee. The guide calls for her to return, but his efforts go unheeded.

When she finally re-emerges on the trail several minutes later, she is out of breath and her face is flushed. She says, 'I require sustainable, environmentally friendly mineral water immediately.' The guide hands her a bottle, which she glugs from greedily. Now slapping the back of her neck with the palm of her hand, she shrieks, 'Oh no! I've been bitten by an insect.' A bottle of insect repellent is extracted from her pocket. When she sprays the mist, the guide splutters.

The guide is pointing into the tree canopy. The ecotourist follows the direction of his finger.

'Wonderful,' she says; 'it's a sloth.'

The ecotourist's drone camera soars upwards and sibilates beside the sloth on a branch. Observing the sloth attempting to flee the drone, the ecotourist says, 'I never knew sloths could move so quickly.'

The pair are about to continue along the trail when a

shimmering, several metres high red force field materialises in front of them, preventing them from progressing any further. The ecotourist says, 'Is this a natural phenomenon?'

'*No señora*. It is God.'

'You mean the Almighty Supercomputer.'

'*Sì,*' says the guide.

'The Almighty Supercomputer must be unaware that I am an ecotourist, here to help the environment.' The ecotourist is tentatively reaching out with her finger towards the force field.

'*¡NO!*' shouts the guide.

'AHHH!' shrieks the ecotourist, rapidly withdrawing her finger. 'It really, really hurts, like an electric shock.'

When the force field starts edging towards them, they flee in the direction from whence they came.

NATIVITY SCENE

FOUR YEARS LATER – DECEMBER 23RD, 2193 AD – WINCHESTER CATHEDRAL – WINCHESTER – Amongst the throng of onlookers viewing the nativity scene is 146-year-old Terrence. He is currently discussing the nativity scene with one of his fellow onlookers.

'For someone my age,' says Terrence, 'it is rather strange seeing the merging of old religious traditions with the new.'

'But new religions have always drawn on those that came before, in't they? Take the Ancient Egyptian god Horus. Born to a virgin on Christmas Day, so they say. No prizes for guessing what happened when the next religion popped up. It's only natural that now we worship Almighty Supercomputer there'll be stuff in it from what came before.'

'I appreciate that. Nonetheless, it is going to take some getting used to, seeing a Commodore 64 in a manger.'

MODERN FAMILY

JULY 11TH, 2194 AD – SOMEWHERE – 'I've got to go; I'm meeting my dad at six,' says the girl to her friend.

'But I thought you said that your dad lives in another country.'

'That's a different dad.'

'A different dad?'

'Yeah. My donor dad lives in another country, but my other dad lives in town since he split with Mum. Where's your dad live?'

'I don't have a dad.'

'Oh, no dad?'

'But I have four mums.'

'Four? Cool! How come?'

'Well, what happened was, before I was born three of my mums were in a polyamorous triad relationship. And then they got married and decided to have a kid, which is me.'

'But you said you have four mums.'

'Yeah. What happened was, my mums … well, my three mums who were in a polyamorous triad relationship that is, realised they weren't good-looking enough to have a kid. So, they hired my fourth mum from this donor agency they found on the holonet. And she agreed to donate her genes, which was so lucky for me because she is really, really pretty and much hotter than my other three mums, who are like really amazing people and super talented, but don't look so great.

'So, I am 25% of my really good-looking mum's genes and 25% of each of my other three mums' genes, which cross my fingers will mean I look fairly hot when I grow up but will also be a really nice person and good at loads of things.'

CONFESSION

MAY 1ST, 2195 AD – ELY CATHEDRAL – ELY, CAMBRIDGESHIRE –
ENGLAND – Terrence is ambling along Ely Cathedral's nave,
admiring the ceiling's 19th-century depictions of stories from the
Bible. The cathedral choir is practising. Terrence stops and listens.

All creatures of our God and King break
Lift up your voice and with us sing, break
Alleluia! Alleluia! break
Thou burning sun with golden beam, break
Thou silver moon with softer gleam! p class equals chorus
Refrain end paragraph

Terrence continues along the nave. At its end he takes a seat on
a bench near the confession booths. A woman on the bench
behind him is speaking in tongues.

'Javascript type = text (date id DEFAULT _) START get time !
function CDATA *) > window #9B18DD COOKIE _ NAME))
var < get Time > #18DD3F) = _ var.'

Terrence shuffles along the bench until he is out of earshot.
Scooting towards him is a robotic bishop, a mitre perched
precariously on its head. Terrence helps himself to a mug of tea
and a chocolate digestive biscuit from the bishop's tray.

When the door of a confession booth slides open, a person
clambers out and cries out jubilantly, 'Font class equals ve5
#C64FBE

Hr

Close font

Font class equals ve5 p'

And then in a flawless tenor, 'Amazing grace! how sweet the
sound, break

That saved a wretch like me! break
I once was lost, but now am found ...'

Job Market

06:30 – JUNE 22ND, 2196 AD – ELY, CAMBRIDGESHIRE – The man sits up in bed, turns off the alarm and yawns. He wishes that he could stay in bed for another hour or two, but today is a working day. So, he clambers out of bed and makes his way to the bathroom. Five minutes later and still in his pyjamas the man is in the kitchen, pouring himself a mug of caffeinated spirulina sea algae. After his morning fix he sets off at a trot in the direction of the house's cellar.

His workaholic wife, having risen early, is already lying in her virtual-reality pod on the cellar floor. The man bends down and opens his waist-high, one-person oval-shaped pod, clambers inside, puts on his VR helmet and lies down. He reaches up and closes the lid. This morning, like every weekday, he is joining his work syndicate. Their current project is a game of virtual-reality neo-Monopoly against a rival team.

He used to be a financial services software operative, but what with the world now being ruled by artificial intelligence he, along with the vast majority of its workforce, was made redundant. Like most people these days, he survives on a small guaranteed income generated by machines.

REALITY

APRIL 28TH, 2197 AD – A CO-OPERATIVE CARE RETIREMENT FACILITY – DOWNHAM MARKET, NORFOLK – ENGLAND – An alarm rings and the lights turn on, revealing a windowless room stacked from floor to ceiling with shelves containing rectangular pods, resembling coffins. When the lids slide open their yawning occupants sit up and rub their eyes. The occupants of the bottom shelf clamber out of their pods, perform some light stretches, put on their dressing gowns and slippers, and leave the room.

A self-driving forklift scoots in and proceeds to remove a pod from the second shelf. It places the pod gently on the floor. When the occupier gets out of the pod the forklift returns the now empty pod to its position on the shelf, before repeating the process with the next pod. On the top shelf, recent arrival, 150-year-old Terrence, is heaving himself out of his pod.

'Warning, F6, remain in your pod,' says the forklift. 'You are in violation of Health and Safety regulation 3ii.'

Terrence sighs, plunks himself back down in the pod. On the shelf below, female resident Cortina, says, 'Some people never learn.'

Terrence grits his teeth.

Ten minutes later – The retirement facility's residents are on the treadmills in the recreation room. Terrence, walking briskly, takes sporadic nibbles from the custard cream biscuit clasped in one hand and gulps from the mug of tea held in his other. A few treadmills down, a man is talking loudly.

'The Inca were a truly remarkable people, their architectural achievements simply outstanding. It is no wonder they were the most successful empire in pre-Columbian America.'

From the treadmill two down from Terrence, Cortina says,

'Stop harkin' on about 'em Incas, will yah?' And now addressing the occupant of the treadmill next to hers, she says, 'Spending all his virtual time with 'em foreign Incas when he could be on a virtual package holiday experience with his own kind. Ridiculous!'

Terrence, increasing his pace, wishes he were on a treadmill further removed from Cortina. The retirement facility's human manager is doing the rounds, an automated assistant following at her heels. The manager is the home's only human employee. When she sees one of her charges standing stationary on his treadmill, the manager says, 'It's important that you keep moving. Your muscles require a workout after all that time spent in your Paradise Pod … There you go. It feels good, doesn't it?'

When the manager draws up alongside Cortina's treadmill, she says, 'Hello, how are you today?'

'Me tooth's been botherin' me a bit,' says Cortina, pulling at the corner of her mouth with her index finger. 'Right back there.'

'Unfortunately, the dental robot is out of order today, but I'll book her in to give you a visit in your pod next week.' The manager bends down and inspects the calendar on the automated assistant at her feet. 'Shall we say Thursday at three?' *Cortina tuts.* 'Is that a yes, Cortina?'

'Yeah.'

When the manager walks off, Terrence hears Cortina say, 'It's an outrage, I'm tellin' yah, that in this day 'n' age dey can't figure aht 'ow to do dental stuff 'n' all dat in virtual time. I could be on the beach in Benidorm drinkin' me tequila sunrise, 'n' the dental thingy could come along and do its business. But no, I 'ave to be interrupted, in't I? It's because of 'em foreigners, I'm telling yah!'

Terrence sighs. A male resident on the treadmill behind him announces, 'I'm going to Greggs to get a sausage roll. Anyone fancy a stroll?'

'Yes, why not,' says Terrence. 'I could do with some fresh air.'

VR

JUNE 30TH, 2198 AD – A PARADISE POD – A CO-OPERATIVE CARE
RETIREMENT FACILITY – DOWNHAM MARKET, NORFOLK –
Terrence is lying on his back with his eyes closed, his arms held at
his sides. But whilst his body is sedentary, his mind is anything
but.

Virtual-reality Terrence is standing on a raised platform.
Behind him is a large audience. Stationed in front of him is the
grinning game show host. The game show host says, 'Are you
ready Terrence?'

'As ready as I will ever be.'

When the game show host clicks his fingers a multitude of
subject names materialise on a large holographic screen beside
him. A cheesy jingle precedes the subject names whizzing around
the screen in all directions. Terrence mutters under his breath,
'Please not sport, please not sport.'

A whooshing sound is followed by the subject names
disappearing with the exception of one, which now expands in
size – *Technology*.

When the game show host sweeps his hand in front of the
screen a multiple-choice question appears – *The first handheld
mobile telephone was produced in which year? – 1891, 1951, 1973
or 1981.*

'1973!'

After a pause *1973* starts flashing green.

'Correct answer; well done!' says the game show host.

The audience applauds.

The jingle is playing again, the subject names are whirring
about in all directions, and Terrence is muttering, 'Please not
sport, please not sport.'

The jingle stops and all the subject names disappear except one, which now expands in size – *Religion*. Under which is a question. *How many books are in the New Testament?* – *18, 21, 23, 27.*

'Um, let me think … um … 27.'

'Is that your final answer Terrence?'

'Yes.'

After a suspenseful pause, *27* flashes green. There is rapturous applause.

'Phew,' says Terrence.

Benidorm

THE SAME DAY – A PARADISE POD – A CO-OPERATIVE CARE RETIREMENT FACILITY – DOWNHAM MARKET, NORFOLK – The haze dissipates, revealing a scantily dressed, tourist-rammed *avenida*. A row of towering concrete buildings runs along one side, a beach the other. So rammed is the beach with holidaymakers that it affords only fleeting glimpses of sand. This is the scene that greets bikini-wearing, 123-year-old Cortina. Driven by a primal urge to join the herd of her fellow countrymen on the beach, she breaks into a trot, causing several drops of the tequila sunrise cocktail she is holding to spill onto her sunburnt belly.

Wedged in by guts protruding above skimpy swimwear, Cortina listens contentedly to the legion of voluminous voices spouting English in a multitude of regional accents. A bevy of shaven-headed, super-strength-cider-glugging youths push through the crowd, an enormous England flag held above their heads.

'*Engaland! Engaland! Engaland!*' they chant.

The patriotic fervour surges through the holidaymakers. Cortina, raising her tequila sunrise above her head, chants, '*Engaland! Engaland! Engaland! En-ga-land!*'

Cortina delights in the chaotic yet predictable nature of the Spanish coastal town of Benidorm during these halcyon days of the package holidaymaker. All day getting smashed, scoffing fish and chips, being roasted red by the sun, only to do it all over again tomorrow and the day after. With the sensations being superficial, Cortina can, health permitting, spend the best part of the next half a century here, living out her retirement, at this her ideal moment in history, before the Eastern Europeans came to Benidorm in droves, before the infestation of drones, before the searing heat, so unbearable today that only the hardiest of Saharan refugees can brave its beaches in summer. Cortina cannot envisage ever swapping her early 1990s Benidorm experience for any of the other virtual-reality options available to her and her fellow retirees in their Paradise Pods.

Leisure Time

THE FOLLOWING DAY – A PARADISE POD – A CO-OPERATIVE CARE RETIREMENT FACILITY – DOWNHAM MARKET, NORFOLK – Subject names are whizzing about the holographic screen in all directions. Terrence crosses his fingers and mutters under his breath, 'Please not sport, please not sport.'

All the subject names disappear, except one, which now expands in size – *The Environment*. A question materialises beneath it – *In what year did China cease being the World's No.1 emitter of CO2?* – *2021, 2035, 2099, 2111.*

'2099!'

'Is that your final answer Terrence?'

'Yes.'

When the word *Correct* appears on the screen the audience applauds and Terrence pumps the air with his fist. This is the furthest he has ever progressed on this virtual-reality game show.

Whilst the subject names whizz about in all directions Terrence mutters, 'Please not sport, please not sport.'

The subjects disappear, apart from one – *Sport.*

'Oh no!'

The question appears on the screen – *In the pre cyberware and anti-ageing medication eras, in which year did Arsenal last win the Champions League?* – *2091, 2096, 2099, Never.*

'Um … um … not the foggiest … Let me think … um.'

'Take your time Terrence.'

'I'm going with … um … *2096.*'

'Is that your final answer Terrence?'

'Y-yes.'

Me-me-meeee … Incorrect.

'Damn!'

The scene disintegrates, and Terrence finds himself back in his Paradise Pod. Having banged the back of his head against his headrest he clenches his fists at his sides. Lying on his back in the darkness Terrence slows his rate of breathing, at the same time as reminding himself that it was only a game and that he will have a chance to do better next time.

A voice emanating from the shelf below says, 'Why they always have to interrupt my Benidorm virtual hols at the best bit?'

'AHHH!'

Carnal Relations

JULY 5TH, 2199 AD – OLYMPIA, WASHINGTON STATE – AMERICA –
Three teenage friends, a girl and two boys, are hanging out in a suburban house in the Olde American speaking state of Washington.

'You get laid this week?' It is the girl who says this.

'Yeah, like three times! One dudette, one dude and a trans dude/dudette.'

'Didn't know you were into that shit *hombre*,' says the other boy, who now pours himself another drink from the keg.

'I like to mix and match *cabrón*, what can I say.'

'*Cool*,' says the girl. 'Me too! This week I got laid twice. Once with this hunk, and the other time with three smoking-hot babes … How about you?'

'Yeah, bro, did you get any action?'

'A *chica*. Slim, dark hair, massive titties.'

'A dick?'

'No dick. A standard *chica*, bro. We did it old skool.'

'What do you mean?'

'Yeah, *holmes*, what is *old skool?*'

'Like old-timer style, as in real, not virtual reality.'

'Oh my Almighty Supercomputer!' shrieks the girl.

'You can't be serious.'

'Yeah, I'm serious.'

'Diseases, *hello*,' says the girl, now pacing up and down the room. 'It's what animals and primitive people from olden times did.'

'Well, *yeah*.'

'I'm so, so grossed out with you right *now*.'

ROCK OF DOOM

SEPTEMBER 2ND, 2200 AD – A BACK GARDEN – LONDON – A man is looking up at space through a telescope. Noticing a rock-like object hurtling downwards through the night sky, he says to his friend, 'It's an asteroid. A big one. Can't be more than a day or two away. It looks like it is heading right this way.'

'Oh no, that would be a disaster. But there's no way the Almighty Supercomputer would allow that to happen, is there?'

'Well, presumably not, but who knows? We'll find out soon enough.'

Apocalypse

TWO DAYS LATER – A SELF-SERVICE RETIREMENT FACILITY – STOWBRIDGE, NORFOLK – ENGLAND – Stretching the length of several fields are rows of transparent, coffin-shaped Paradise Pods, above which a blood-red moon gleams in a cloud-clustered sky. Every second pod starts flashing blue. Moments later their lids slide open and elderly people emerge, sitting up in their Paradise Pods, stretching out, yawning, and extracting the sustenance drips from their forearms.

Having put on his dressing gown, 153-year-old Terrence hauls himself out of his pod, slips on his wellington boots and stretches out his aged limbs. Despite being on muscle rejuvenation medication, he requires a fair bit of limbering up these days.

Terrence bends down and pulls out the two hosepipes from the underside of his pod – one for waste, the other for sustenance. With a hose held in each hand he joins his fellow retirees, trudging across the field towards their nearest communal area. Last year Terrence transferred to this self-service retirement facility, which is but a short distance from his former retirement facility. He likes the sense of independence this place affords.

When Terrence reaches the communal area, he inserts the nozzle of his waste hose into the sewage tank, presses the extract button and then waits for the waste to be vacuumed into the tank. Looking up, he notes the dark ominous sky, the blood-red moon and the billowing pillars of cloud. It is quite unlike anything he has witnessed before. A man approaches the sewage tank, inserts the nozzle of his hose through one of its openings and says in a Brummie accent, 'Or-lando Disney-land were amaz-ing, absol-utely fan-tastic.'

'Look at the sky,' says Terrence, pointing upwards. 'Something big is happening.'

Having glanced upwards, the man says, 'The rides at Or-lando are amaz-ing. Ma-gic moun-tain …'

But Terrence is not listening, for he is looking across the flat fields at the banks of the River Great Ouse, above which seagulls swarm in all directions, squawking incessantly. A wave spills over the bank, showering the adjoining field. Close by to where he stands, four horses come galloping past.

'Apocalypse,' says Terrence.

The man glances in the direction of the horses. He says, '*Space Moun-tain* were brilliant.'

When the waste matter has been vacuumed away, the two men remove the nozzles of their hoses from the sewage tank and head over to the sustenance tank. As liquid green spirulina sea algae is sucked into the pipe, Terrence stares up at the heavens. Meanwhile, his fellow retiree says, 'I fancy a kipper tie.' Having lodged his waste pipe under one armpit, his sustenance pipe under the other, he traipses over to a drink vending machine and selects a cup of tea.

An elderly woman who resides two pods down from Terrence is inserting her waste hose into the tank. She says, 'Wha' yer gorpin at Terrence?'

'The sky. It is remarkably dark for daytime. And you can see the moon. Look, it is as red as blood. And the clouds look like billowing pillars of smoke. My bet is an asteroid has hit Earth. Everything is pointing to this being the Apocalypse.'

'An' yisterday wuz wet, an' orl.'

It is becoming darker, the moon yet redder, and Terrence realises that what he thought were pillars of cloud littering the sky are actually thick plumes of smoke. The other people in the communal area are oblivious as they refuel, drink tea and chatter about their virtual-reality experiences. But then an Oriental lady, pointing upwards, shrieks, '*Pahayag!*'

'Paha *what?*' says someone.

'*Pahayag* mus' be furrin' far Apoc-alypse,' says the woman who resides two pods down from Terrence.

Everyone is traipsing back towards their pods, trailing their hosepipes behind them. When the four horses come galloping past again, Terrence says, 'The Apocalypse is upon us.'

'For Gawd's searke,' says Terrence's neighbour, 'gi yar tongue a rest an' stop goin' on about the Apoc-alypse. Yew do run on, an' thas a fact!'

Everyone clambers back into their virtual-reality pods. Having reattached their sustenance drips to their forearms, they lie down and pull their pods lids closed.

But Terrence does not get back in his pod. Instead he stands, peering upwards at the pillars of smoke billowing in the sky. The pods on either side of him start flashing blue, signifying that it is time for their occupants to refuel.

20 MINUTES LATER – 'It's the Apocalypse!' shouts Terrence.

'Stop houndin' us, will yah?' says an elderly man, who having clambered into his Paradise Pod pulls the lid abruptly down on top of him.

Terrence, prodding upwards with his finger, shouts, 'Look at the sky. The Apocalypse is upon us!'

A woman, sitting in her pod, reattaching her sustenance drip to the underside of her wrist, says, 'Get lost, you loon!'

Across the fields Terrence sees water surging over the riverbank, above which swarming seagulls squawk loudly in a sky littered with towering plumes of billowing smoke.

'It's the Apocalypse!'

A retiree, reattaching the wastepipe to the bottom of their pod, says, 'Piss off!'

'But it is the Apocalypse. The World is ending.'

'Well, it's a good thing I'm gettin' back to virtual-reality world, then innit? Now bugger off!'

Terrence hurries over to a woman, poised to get into her pod. He says, 'The Apocalypse is upon us!'

'*Kuring teu ngarti.* No speake Englishe.'

With everyone back in their Paradise Pods, Terrence is alone.

CRASH! The riverbank bursts. Terrence, rapping on Paradise Pod lids, shouts, 'Get out! The Apocalypse is here!'

But the occupants' minds have returned to their virtual-reality worlds, and they are oblivious. Water is surging across the fields towards the self-service retirement facility. Terrence departs in the opposite direction as fast as his aged legs will carry him.

NINE HOURS LATER – Terrence had been up to his chin in floodwater when the unoccupied pedalo (paddle boat) came drifting past. With considerable effort Terrence had managed to haul himself aboard. He has since been carried on the water several miles and is currently bobbing up and down above Downham Market, the town where his previous retirement facility was situated.

Terrence is looking up at the pillars of smoke billowing in the sky when he hears a voice calling, 'Oi, over 'ere!'

Terrence is looking all around him.

'Over 'ere!'

Floundering close by in the water, clutching onto a plank, is an elderly woman. Terrence pedals over to the woman, who now shouts, 'Get a move on Terrence, will yah?'

Terrence hauls Cortina aboard the pedalo.

'Bloody 'ell, what's goin' on? Why's water everywhere, and what's up with the sky?'

'There has been an Apocalypse.'

'Oh *yeah!*'

'Caused presumably by an asteroid hitting Earth.'

'Oh! So, it weren't global warming that got us in the end.'

'Seemingly not.'

'Why ain't the Almighty Supercomputer done nothin' abaht it? If it's so powerful an' all, why don't it stop it?'

'Haven't the foggiest. Maybe it was powerless to, or was not programmed to. It must have been our destiny. An asteroid apparently wiped out the dinosaurs. It was our turn this time ... Life as we know it may continue in some capacity, on Mars maybe. Who knows.'

'Well, a fat load of good that's goin' to do us!' Cortina goes on to explain what happened to her. 'I was on my virtual package hols when the dental robot thingamajig woke me up to do some work on me tooth. Then all this water started floodin' in. Everyone else were sleepin', dreamin' in their virtual worlds; you know how they are ...'

While Cortina drones on, Terrence surveys the sky and the endless water stretching to the horizon. An old, rusted ship comes into view. There are numerous birds perched on its deck.

'Maybe it's an ark, like Noah's Ark in the Bible,' says Terrence. 'If and when the waters recede the creatures on that boat might repopulate the Earth.'

'Good for them! What abaht me, 'eh? 'Ow am I goin' to get back to Benidorm?'

The End

Please consider leaving a review for Tomorrow's World on Amazon/Goodreads or elsewhere.

If you liked Tomorrow's World you might enjoy my humorous, monthly book-related newsletter – http://eepurl.com/btLcrX

www.ingramcontent.com/pod-product-compliance
Lightning Source LLC
Chambersburg PA
CBHW020513120726
47904CB00003B/814